REBEL, I

(OF CROWNS AND GLORY—BOOK 4)

MORGAN RICE

Books by Morgan Rice

THE WAY OF STEEL
ONLY THE WORTHY (BOOK #1)

VAMPIRE, FALLEN
BEFORE DAWN (BOOK #1)

OF CROWNS AND GLORY
SLAVE, WARRIOR, QUEEN (BOOK #1)
ROGUE, PRISONER, PRINCESS (BOOK #2)
KNIGHT, HEIR, PRINCE (BOOK #3)
REBEL, PAWN, KING (BOOK #4)
SOLDIER, BROTHER SORCERER (BOOK #5)

KINGS AND SORCERERS
RISE OF THE DRAGONS
RISE OF THE VALIANT
THE WEIGHT OF HONOR
A FORGE OF VALOR
A REALM OF SHADOWS
NIGHT OF THE BOLD

THE SORCERER'S RING
A QUEST OF HEROES
A MARCH OF KINGS
A FATE OF DRAGONS
A CRY OF HONOR
A VOW OF GLORY
A CHARGE OF VALOR
A RITE OF SWORDS
A GRANT OF ARMS
A SKY OF SPELLS
A SEA OF SHIELDS
A REIGN OF STEEL
A LAND OF FIRE
A RULE OF QUEENS
AN OATH OF BROTHERS
A DREAM OF MORTALS
A JOUST OF KNIGHTS
THE GIFT OF BATTLE

CHAPTER ONE

Thanos felt a pit in his stomach as the ship rocked its way across the sea, each passing current taking him farther and farther from home. There had been no land in sight for days now. He stood at the prow of the boat, looking out at the water, waiting for the moment when he would finally spy something. Only the thought of what might lie ahead, *who* might lie ahead, kept him from ordering the captain to turn the ship around.

Ceres.

She was out there somewhere, and he would find her.

"You sure about this?" the captain asked, coming up beside him. "No one I know wants to take a trip to the Isle of Prisoners."

What could Thanos say to that? That he didn't know? That he felt a bit like the boat, pushed forward by its oars even as the wind tried to push it back?

The need to find Ceres, though, surpassed everything else. It drove Thanos, filling him with excitement at the prospect of finding her. He'd been so sure that she was gone, that he would never see her again. When he'd heard that she might be alive, the relief had flooded him, had made him feel as though he might collapse.

Yet he could not deny that thoughts of Stephania were there too, making him glance back, and even, for a flash, think about *going* back. She was his wife, after all, and he'd abandoned her. She was carrying his child, and he'd walked away. He'd left her there on the docks. What kind of man did that?

"She tried to kill me," Thanos reminded himself.

"What's that?" the captain asked, and Thanos realized he'd said it aloud.

"Nothing," Thanos said. He sighed. "The truth is that I don't know. I'm looking for someone, and the Isle of Prisoners is the only place she might have gone."

He knew Ceres's ship had sunk on the way to the island. If she'd survived, then it made sense that she might have made it there, didn't it? That explained why Thanos hadn't seen anything of her since, too. If she'd been able to get back to him, Thanos had to believe that she would have.

"Seems an awfully big risk to take for not knowing," the captain said.

"She's worth it," Thanos assured him.

"She must be something special to be better than Lady Stephania," the smuggler said with a leer that made Thanos want to punch him.

1

"That's my wife you're talking about," Thanos said, and even he recognized the obvious problem with that. He couldn't defend her when he was the one who had left her behind, and when she'd been the one to order his death. She probably deserved everything anyone said about her.

Now, if only he could convince himself of that. If only his thoughts of Ceres didn't continue to be punctuated by thoughts of Stephania, as she'd been with him at the castle feasts, as she'd been in quiet moments, as she'd looked on the morning after their wedding night…

"Are you sure you can get me onto the Isle of Prisoners safely?" Thanos asked. He'd never been there, but the whole island was meant to be a well-guarded fortress of a place, inescapable for those who were brought there.

"Oh, that's easy enough," the captain assured him. "We go by there sometimes. The guards sell some of the prisoners they've broken as slaves. String them up on poles on the shore for us to see as we get close."

Thanos had long since decided that he hated this man. He hid it, though, because right then the smuggler was the only chance he had to get to the island and find Ceres.

"I don't exactly want to run into the guards," he pointed out.

The other man shrugged. "That's easy enough. We get close, drop you in a small boat, and keep going like it's a normal visit. Then we'll wait off the coast for you. Not long, mind you. Wait too long, and they might think we're doing something suspicious."

Thanos had no doubt that the smuggler would abandon him given any threat to his ship. Only the prospect of profit had brought him this far. A man like this wouldn't understand love. For him, it was probably something you hired on the docks by the hour. But he'd gotten Thanos this far. That was what mattered.

"You realize that even if you find this woman on the Isle of Prisoners," the captain said, "she might not be the way you remember."

"Ceres will always be Ceres," Thanos insisted.

He heard the other man snort. "Easy enough to say, but you don't know the things they do there. Some of the ones they sell us as slaves, there's barely enough of them left to do anything for themselves unless we tell them."

"And I'm sure you're happy to," Thanos snapped back.

"Don't like me much, do you?" the captain asked.

Thanos ignored the question, staring out to sea. They both knew the answer, and right then, he had better things to think about. He had to find a way to locate Ceres, whatever that—

"Is that land?" he asked, pointing.

It was no more than a dot on the horizon at first, but even like that, it looked bleak, surrounded by clouds and with roiling waves. As it grew closer, Thanos could feel a sense of brooding dread growing in him.

The island rose up in a series of gray granite spikes like the teeth of some great beast. A bastion sat on the topmost point of the island, a lighthouse above it burning constantly, as if to warn away all who might come there. Thanos could see trees on one side of the island, but most of it seemed to be bare.

As they came closer still, he could see windows that seemed to be carved straight into the rock of the island, as if the whole place had been hollowed out to make the prison bigger. He saw shale beaches too, with bleached white bones sticking out against them. Thanos heard shrieks, and he paled at the realization that he couldn't tell if they were sea birds or people.

Thanos slid his small boat up the shale of the beach, wincing with disgust at the sight of manacles set there below the tide line. His imagination told him immediately what they were for: torturing or executing prisoners using the incoming waves. A set of abandoned bones on the shore told their own story.

The captain of the smuggling boat turned to him and smiled.

"Welcome to the Isle of Prisoners."

CHAPTER TWO

To Stephania, the world felt bleak without Thanos there. It felt cold, despite the warmth of the sun. Empty, despite the bustle of people around the castle. She stared out over the city, and she could have happily burned it all down, because none of it meant anything. All she could do was sit by the windows of her rooms, feeling as though someone had ripped out her heart.

Maybe someone still would. She'd risked everything for Thanos, after all. What was the precise penalty for assisting a traitor? Stephania knew the answer to that, because it was the same as everything else in the Empire: whatever the king decided. She had little doubt that he would want her death for this.

One of her handmaids offered her a soothing herbal tonic. Stephania ignored it, even when the girl set it down on a small stone table beside her.

"My lady," the girl said. "Some of the others... they're wondering... shouldn't we be making preparations to leave the city?"

"To leave the city," Stephania said. She could hear how flat and stupid her own voice sounded.

"It's just... aren't we in danger? With everything that's happened, and all you had us do... to help Thanos."

"Thanos!" The name shocked her out of her stupor for a moment, and anger followed in its wake. Stephania picked up the herbal concoction. "Don't you dare mention his name, you stupid girl! Get out. Get *out*!"

Stephania threw the cup with its steaming brew. Her handmaid ducked, which was irritating in itself, but the sound of the cup shattering more than made up for it. Brown liquid spilled down the wall. Stephania ignored it.

"No one is to disturb me!" she yelled after the girl. "Or I'll have your skin for it."

Stephania needed to be alone with her thoughts, even if they were such dark thoughts that a part of her wanted to throw herself from the balcony of the rooms just to end it all. Thanos was gone. All she'd done, all she'd worked for, and Thanos was gone. She'd never believed in love before him; she'd been convinced it was a weakness that only opened you up to pain, but with him it had seemed worth the risk. Now, it turned out that she'd been right. Love only made it easier for the world to hurt you.

Stephania heard the sound of the door opening, and she whirled again, looking for something else to throw.

4

"I said I wasn't to be disturbed!" she snapped, before she saw who it was.

"That's hardly very grateful," Lucious said as he walked in, "when I had you escorted back here so carefully to ensure your safety."

Lucious was dressed like some storybook prince, in white velvet worked with gold designs and gemstones. He had his dagger at his belt, but he'd removed his golden armor and his sword. Even his hair looked freshly cleaned, free of any taint of the city. He looked, to Stephania, more like a man ready to sing songs beneath her window than one organizing the defense of the city.

"Escorted," Stephania said with a tight smile. "That's one word for it."

"I ensured you traveled safely through the war-torn streets of our city," Lucious said, "my men seeing that you didn't fall prey to rebels, or find yourself kidnapped by that murderous husband of yours. Did you know he'd escaped?"

Stephania frowned. What game was Lucious playing?

"Of course I know," Stephania snapped back. She stood, because she didn't like Lucious looming over her. "I was there."

She saw Lucious raise an eyebrow in mock surprise. "Why, Stephania, are you admitting to some role in your husband's escape? Because none of the evidence points that way."

Stephania looked at him levelly. "What did you do?"

"I did nothing," Lucious said, obviously enjoying this far too much. "In fact, I've been arduously seeking out the truth of the matter. *Most* arduously."

Which, for Lucious, meant torturing people. Stephania had no objection to cruelty, but she certainly didn't take the pleasure in it that he did.

She sighed. "Stop playing games, Lucious. What have you done?"

Lucious shrugged. "I've seen to it that things work out the way I want," he said. "When I speak to my father, I will tell him that Thanos killed a number of guards on the way out, while another admitted to assisting because of rebel sympathies. Sadly, he did not survive to tell his story again. A weak heart."

Lucious clearly made sure that no one who had seen Stephania there survived. Even Stephania felt disgust at the callousness of it, although there was another part of her already working out what it meant for her in the context of everything else.

"Sadly, it seems that one of your handmaids was caught up in the plot," Lucious said. "Thanos seduced her, it seems."

Anger flashed through Stephania then. "They are *my* handmaidens!"

It wasn't just the thought of women who'd served her so loyally being hurt, though that was bad enough. It was the thought that Lucious would dare to harm someone who was so obviously *hers*. It wasn't just the thought of one of one of those who served her being harmed, it was the insult of it!

"And that was the point," Lucious said. "Too many people had seen her about your errands. And when I offered the girl her life in exchange for everything she knew, she was most helpful."

Stephania looked away. "Why do all this, Lucious? You could have left me to go with Thanos."

"Thanos didn't *deserve* you," Lucious said. "He certainly didn't deserve to be happy."

"And why did you cover up my role in it?" Stephania asked. "You could have stood back and watched me executed."

"I did think about it," Lucious admitted. "Or at least, I thought about asking the king for you when we told him. But there was too much of a chance of him simply executing you out of hand, and we couldn't have that."

Only Lucious would speak about something like that so openly, or thought that Stephania was just something he could ask his father for like some precious bauble. Just the thought of it made Stephania's skin crawl.

"But then it occurred to me," Lucious said, "that I am enjoying the game between us far too much to do something like that. It isn't the way I want you, anyway. I want you to be my equal, my partner. Truly mine."

Stephania stepped over to the balcony, as much for fresh air as anything. This close, Lucious's scent was of expensive rose water and perfumes obviously designed to disguise the blood beneath from the rest of his day's exertions.

"What are you saying?" Stephania asked, although she already had a good idea of some of what Lucious would want from her. She'd made it her business to find out everything there was to know about the others at court, including Lucious's appetites.

Although maybe she hadn't done such a good job of it. She hadn't realized that Lucious had been worming his way into her network of informants and spies. She hadn't learned about the things Thanos was doing either, until it had been too late.

She couldn't compare the two though. Lucious was utterly without morals or stopping points, actively seeking out new ways to hurt others. Thanos was strong and principled, loving and protective.

But he'd been the one to leave her. He'd abandoned her, knowing what might happen afterwards.

Lucious reached out for her hand, taking it in a grip that was gentler than anything he normally managed. Even so, Stephania had to fight the urge to cringe as he lifted her hand to his lips, kissing the inside of her wrist, right where the pulse throbbed.

"Lucious," Stephania said, pulling her hand away. "I'm a married woman."

"I've rarely found that to be a barrier," Lucious pointed out. "And let's be honest, Stephania, I doubt you have either."

Stephania's anger flared up again then. "You know nothing about me."

"I know everything about you," Lucious said. "And the more I see, the more I know that you and I are perfect for one another."

Stephania walked away, but Lucious followed. Of course he did. He wasn't a man who had ever been denied.

"Think about it, Stephania," Lucious said. "I thought you were nothing but empty headed, but then I learned about the spider's web you've woven in Delos. You know what I felt then?"

"Anger that you'd been made a fool of?" Stephania suggested.

"Careful," Lucious said. "You wouldn't want me angry with you. No, I felt admiration. Before, I thought you might be good to bed for a night or two. Afterwards, I thought you might be someone who truly understood how the world works."

Oh, Stephania understood, better than someone like Lucious could ever know. He had his position to protect him from whatever the world threw at him. Stephania had only her cleverness.

"And you decided we would be the perfect match," Stephania said. "Tell me then, what did you plan to do about my marriage to Thanos?"

"These things can be put aside," Lucious said, as if it were as simple as snapping his fingers. "After what he's done, I would have thought you'd be happy to be free of *that* attachment."

There would be an advantage to having the priests do it, because otherwise Stephania risked being tarnished with Thanos's crimes. She would always be the woman married to the traitor, even if Lucious had ensured that no one would ever be able to tie her to the crimes.

"Or, if you don't want that," Lucious said, "I'm sure it won't take much to ensure his demise. After all, you so nearly managed it before. Regardless of where he's gone, another assassin could be arranged. You could mourn for a… suitable period. I'm sure black would suit you. You look so lovely in everything else."

There was something about Lucious's look that made Stephania uncomfortable, as though he were trying to guess what she would look like without wearing anything at all. She looked him straight in the eyes, trying to keep her tone businesslike.

"And then what?" she demanded.

"And then you marry a more suitable prince," Lucious said. "Think of all we could do together, with the things you know, and the things I can do. We could rule the Empire together, and the rebellion would never even touch us. You have to admit, we would make a lovely couple."

Stephania laughed then. She couldn't help herself. "No, Lucious. We wouldn't, because I don't feel a thing for you beyond contempt. You're a thug, and worse, you're the reason I've lost everything. Why would I ever consider marrying you?"

She watched Lucious's face turn hard.

"I could make you," Lucious pointed out. "I could make you do whatever I want. Do you think I couldn't still let your part in Thanos's escape be known? Maybe I kept that handmaid of yours, for insurance."

"Trying to force me into marriage?" Stephania said. What kind of man would do that?

Lucious spread his hands. "You're not so unlike me, Stephania. You play the game. You wouldn't want some fool coming to you with flowers and jewels. Besides, you'd learn to love me. Whether you wanted to or not."

He reached out for her again, and Stephania put her hand on his chest. "Touch me, and you won't leave this room alive."

"Do you *want* me to reveal your part in helping Thanos escape?" he asked.

"You forget your own part," Stephania said. "After all, you knew all about it. How would the king react if I told him that?"

She expected anger from Lucious then, maybe even violence. Instead, she saw him smile.

"I knew you were perfect for me," he said. "Even in your position, you find a way to fight back, and beautifully. Together, there will be nothing we can't do. It will take you time to realize that though, I know that. You've been through a lot."

He sounded exactly the way a concerned suitor should, which only made Stephania trust him less.

"Take the time to think about everything I've said," Lucious said. "Think about everything a marriage to me could offer you.

8

Certainly compared to being the woman who was married to a traitor. You might not love me yet, but people like us don't make decisions based on that kind of foolishness. We make them because we are superior, and we recognize those like us when we see them."

Stephania was nothing like Lucious, but she knew better than to say it. She just wanted him to go.

"In the meantime," Lucious said when she didn't answer, "I have a gift for you. That handmaiden of yours thought you might need it. She told me all *kinds* of things about you when she was begging for her life."

He drew a vial from his belt pouch, setting it down on the small table by the window.

"She told me about the reason you had to run from the blood moon festival," Lucious said. "About your pregnancy. Clearly, I could never bring up Thanos's child. Drink this, and there will be no issue. In any sense."

Stephania wanted to fling the vial at him. She picked it up to do just that, but he was already out the door.

She went to throw it anyway, but stopped herself, sitting back down at the window and staring at it.

It was clear, the sunlight shining through it in a way that made it seem far more innocent than it was. Drink this, and she would be free to marry Lucious, which was a horrible thought. Yet it would put her in one of the most powerful positions in the Empire. Drink this, and the last remnant of Thanos would be gone.

Stephania sat there, not knowing what to do, and slowly, the tears started to roll down her cheeks.

Maybe she would drink it after all.

CHAPTER THREE

Ceres fought desperately up toward consciousness, pushing through the veils of blackness that pinned her down, like a drowning woman flailing up through water. Even now, she could hear the screams of the dying. The ambush. The battle. She had to force herself to wake, or it would all be lost....

Her eyes snapped open, and she surged to her feet, ready to continue the fight. She tried to, anyway. Something caught at her wrists and ankles, holding her back. Sleep finally fled from her and Ceres saw where she was.

Stone walls surrounded her, curving in a space barely large enough for Ceres to lie down in. There was no bed, just a hard stone floor. A small window set with bars let in light. Ceres could feel the restrictive weight of steel around her wrists and ankles, and she could see the heavy bracket where chains connected her to the wall, the thick door bound with iron bands that proclaimed her a prisoner. The chain disappeared through a slot in the door, suggesting that she could be pulled back from outside, right to the bracket, to pin her against the wall.

Anger filled Ceres then at being caught there like that. She pulled at the bracket, trying to simply yank it from the wall with the strength her powers gave her. Nothing happened.

It was as though there was a fog inside her head, and she was trying to look through it to the landscape beyond. Here and there, the light of memory seemed to break through that fog, but it was a fragmented thing.

She could remember the gates to the city opening, the "rebels" waving them inside. Charging down there, throwing everything into what they'd thought would be the key battle for the city.

Ceres slumped back. She hurt, and some wounds were deeper than just the physical ones.

"Someone betrayed us," Ceres said softly.

They'd been on the verge of victory, and someone had betrayed all of that. Because of money, or fear, or the need for power, someone had given away everything they'd worked for, and left them riding into a trap.

Ceres remembered then. She remembered the sight of Lord West's nephew with an arrow sticking from his throat, the look of helplessness and disbelief that had crossed his face before he'd toppled from the saddle.

She remembered arrows blotting out the sun, and barricades, and fire.

Lord West's men had tried to fire back at the archers assailing them. Ceres had seen their skills as horse archers on the ride to Delos, able to hunt with small bows and fire at a full gallop if they needed to. When they'd fired their first arrows in response, Ceres had even dared to feel hope, because it seemed as though these men would be able to overcome anything.

They hadn't. With Lucious's archers hidden on the rooftops, they'd been at too much of a disadvantage. Somewhere in the chaos, fire pots had joined the arrows, and Ceres had felt the horror of it as she'd seen men start to burn. Only Lucious would have used fire as a weapon in his own city, not caring if the flames spread to the surrounding houses. Ceres had seen horses rearing, men thrown as their mounts panicked.

Ceres should have been able to save them. She'd had reached for the power within her and found only emptiness, a bleak gap where there should have been ready strength and the power to destroy her foes.

She'd still been searching for it when her horse had bucked, sending her tumbling…

Ceres forced her mind back to the present, because there were some places her memory didn't want to linger. The present wasn't much better though, because outside, Ceres could hear the screams of a man who was obviously dying.

Ceres made her way to the window, fighting her way to the very limits of what her chains would allow. Even that was an effort. She felt as though something had scoured her inside, wiping away any of the strength that she might have had. It felt as though she could barely stand then, let alone fight her way clear of the chains that held her.

She managed to get there, wrapping her hands around the bars as if she might pull them out. In truth, though, they were almost the only thing holding her up right then. When she looked down at the courtyard that lay beyond her new cell, she needed that support.

Ceres saw Lord West's men there, standing in line after line of soldiers. Each still wore the remains of his armor, although in many cases pieces of it had been broken or torn from them, and none had their weapons. They had their hands bound, and many were kneeling. There was something sad about that sight. It spoke of their defeat more clearly than almost anything else could have.

Ceres recognized others there, rebels, and the sight of those faces brought an even more visceral reaction. Lord West's men had come with her willingly. They'd risked their lives for her, and Ceres felt responsibility for that, but the men and women below were ones she knew.

She saw Anka. Anka was tied at the heart of it all, her arms strapped behind her to a post, high enough that she couldn't possibly sit or kneel to rest. A rope at throat level threatened to start choking her every time she dared to relax. Ceres could see the blood on her face, left there casually, as if she didn't matter at all.

The sight of it all was enough to make Ceres feel sick. They were friends, people whom Ceres had known for years in some cases. Some of them were wounded. A flash of anger ran through Ceres at that, because no one was trying to help them. Instead, they knelt or stood, the same way the soldiers did.

Then there was the sight of the things they were waiting by. Ceres didn't know what many of them were for, but she could guess, based on the rest. There were impaling poles and blocks for beheading, gallows, and braziers with hot irons. And more. So much more that Ceres could barely begin to comprehend the mind that could decide to do all this.

Then she saw Lucious there amongst them, and she knew. This was down to him, and in a way, down to her. If only she'd been quicker chasing him down when he'd issued his challenge. If only she'd found some way to kill him before this.

Lucious stood over the soldier who was screaming, twisting a sword thrust through him to bring a fresh sound of agony from him. Ceres could see a small crowd of black-hooded torturers and executioners around him, looking on as though taking notes, or possibly just appreciating someone with a twisted flare for their profession. Ceres wished that she could reach out and kill all of them.

Lucious looked up, and Ceres felt the moment when his eyes met hers. It was something akin to the kind of thing bards sang about, with lovers' eyes meeting across a room, only here, there was only hatred. Right then, Ceres would have killed Lucious in any way she could, and she could see what he had in store for her.

She saw his smile spread slowly across his features, and he gave the sword one final twist, his eyes still on Ceres, before he straightened up, wiping bloodied hands absently on a cloth. He stood there like an actor about to deliver a speech to a waiting audience. To Ceres, he simply looked like a butcher.

"Every man and woman here is a traitor to the Empire," Lucious declared. "But I think we all know that it is not your fault.

You have been misled. Corrupted by others. Corrupted by one in particular."

Ceres saw him shoot another look in her direction.

"So I am going to offer mercy to the ordinary ones among you. Crawl to me. Beg to be enslaved, and you will be permitted to live. The Empire always needs more drudges."

No one moved. Ceres didn't know whether to be proud or to scream at them to take the offer. After all, they had to know what was coming.

"No?" Lucious said, and there was a hint of surprise in his tone. Perhaps, Ceres thought, he genuinely had expected everyone there to willingly give themselves over into enslavement to save their lives. Perhaps he really didn't understand what the rebellion was about, or that there were some things worse than death. "No one?"

Ceres saw the pretense of calm control slip away from him then like a mask, revealing what lay beneath.

"This is what happens when you fools start listening to scum who want to mislead you!" Lucious said. "You forget your places! You forget that there are consequences for everything you peasants do! Well, I'm going to remind you that there are consequences. You're going to die, every last one of you, and you're going to do it in ways that people will whisper about every time they so much as think of betraying their betters. And, to make sure of it, I'm going to bring your families here to watch. I'm going to burn them out of their pitiful hovels, and I'm going to make them pay attention while you scream!"

He would do it, too; Ceres had no doubt of that. She saw him point at one of the soldiers, then at one of the devices that were waiting.

"Start with this one. Start with any of them. I don't care. Just make sure that they all suffer before they die." He pointed a finger up toward Ceres's cell. "And make sure that she's last. Make her watch every last one of them die. I want her driven mad by it. I want her to understand just how helpless she really is, no matter how much of the blood of the Ancient Ones she boasts about to her men."

Ceres threw herself back from the bars then, but there must have been men waiting on the other side of the door, because the chains at her wrists and ankles went tight, dragging her back to the wall and spreading her out so that she couldn't move more than an inch or two in any direction. She certainly couldn't look away from the window, through which she could see one of the executioners checking the sharpness of an axe.

"No," she said, trying to fill herself with a confidence she didn't feel right then. "No, I won't let this happen. I'll find a way to stop it."

She didn't just reach into herself then, looking for her power. She dove down into the space where she would normally have found the energy waiting for her. Ceres forced herself to go after the state of mind she'd learned from the Forest Folk. She hunted after the power that she'd gained as surely as if she were chasing after some hidden animal.

Yet it remained as elusive as one. Ceres tried everything she could think of. She tried to calm herself. She tried to remember the sensations that had been there before when she had used her power. She tried forcing it to flow through her with an effort of will. In desperation, Ceres even tried pleading with it, coaxing it as though it were truly some separate being, rather than just a fragment of herself.

None of it worked, and Ceres threw herself against the chains holding her. She felt them bite into her wrists and ankles as she threw herself forward, but she couldn't succeed in gaining so much as an arm's length of space.

Ceres should have been able to snap the steel easily. She should have been able to break free and save all of those there. She should have, but right then, she couldn't, and the worst part was that she didn't even know why. Why had powers she'd already used so much abandoned her so suddenly? Why had it come to this?

Why couldn't she make it do what she wanted? Ceres felt tears touch the edges of her eyes as she fought desperately to be able to do something. To be able to help.

Outside, the executions began, and Ceres couldn't do anything to stop them.

Worse, she knew that when Lucious was done with those outside, it would be her turn next.

CHAPTER FOUR

Sartes woke, ready to fight. He tried to stand, thrashed when he couldn't, and found himself shoved back down by the boot of a rough-looking figure opposite.

"Think there's room for you moving about in here?" he snapped.

The man was shaven-headed and tattooed, missing a finger from some brawl or other. There was a time when Sartes would probably have felt a thrill of fear at seeing a man like that. That was before the army, though, and the rebellion that had followed. It was before he'd seen what real evil looked like.

There were other men there, crammed into a wooden walled space, with light let in only through a few cracks. It was enough for Sartes to see them by, and what he saw was a long way from encouraging. The man opposite him was probably one of the least rough looking there, and the sheer number of them meant that for a moment, Sartes did feel fear, and not just because of what they could do to him. What could be in store if he was stuck in a space with men like this?

He could feel the sensation of movement, and Sartes risked turning his back on the crowd of thugs so that he could look out through one of the cracks in the wooden walls. Outside, he saw a dusty, rocky landscape going past. He didn't recognize the area, but how far away from Delos could he be?

"A cart," he said. "We're in a cart."

"Listen to the boy," the shaven-headed man said. He performed a rough approximation of Sartes's voice, twisted out of all recognition. "We're on a cart. Regular genius this boy is. Well, genius, how about you keep your mouth shut? Bad enough we're on our way to the tar pits without you going on."

"The tar pits?" Sartes said, and he saw a flash of anger cross the other man's face.

"Thought I told you to be quiet," the thug snapped. "Maybe if I shove a few of your teeth down your throat, it will remind you."

Another man stretched. The confined space seemed barely big enough to hold him. "Only one I hear talking is you. How about you both shut up?"

The speed with which the shaven-headed man did it told Sartes a lot about how dangerous this other man was. Sartes doubted that it was a moment that had made him any friends, but he knew from the army that men like this didn't have friends: they had hangers-on and they had victims.

It was hard to be quiet now that he knew where they were going. The tar pits were one of the worst punishments the Empire had; so dangerous and unpleasant that those sent there would be lucky to live out a year. They were hot, deadly places, where the bones of dead dragons could be seen sticking from the ground, and the guards thought nothing of throwing a sick or collapsing prisoner into the tar.

Sartes tried to remember how he'd gotten there. He'd been scouting for the rebellion, trying to find a gate that would let Ceres into the city with Lord West's men. He'd found it. Sartes could remember the elation that he'd felt then, because it had been perfect. He'd raced back to try to tell the others.

He'd been so close when the cloaked figure had grabbed him; close enough that he'd felt as though he could reach out and touch the entrance to the rebellion's hideaway. He'd felt as though he was finally safe, and they'd snatched it away from him.

"Lady Stephania sends her regards."

The words echoed in Sartes's memory. They'd been the last words he heard before they'd struck him unconscious. They'd simultaneously told him who was doing this and that he had failed. They'd let him get that close and then taken it away.

They'd left Ceres and the others without the information Sartes had been able to find. He found himself worrying about his sister, his father, Anka, and the rebellion, not knowing what would happen to them without the gate he'd been able to find for them. Would they be able to get into the city without his help?

Had they been able to do it, Sartes corrected himself, because by now, one way or another, it would be done. They would have found another gate, or an alternative way into the city, wouldn't they? They had to have done, because what was the alternative?

Sartes didn't want to think about that, but it was impossible to avoid. The alternative was that they might have failed. At best, they might have realized that there was no way in without taking a gate, and found themselves trapped there while the army advanced. At worst… at worst, they might already be dead.

Sartes shook his head. He wouldn't believe that. He couldn't. Ceres would find a way to come through it all, and to win. Anka was as resourceful as anyone he'd met. His father was strong and solid, while the other rebels had the determination that came with knowing that their cause was a righteous one. They would find a way to prevail.

Sartes had to think that what was happening to him would be temporary too. The rebels would win, which meant that they would capture Stephania and she would tell them what she'd done. They would come for him, the way his father and Anka had come when he'd been stuck in the army camp.

But what a place they'd have to come to. Sartes looked out as the cart jolted its way across the landscape, and saw the flatness of it give way to pits and rocky surrounds, bubbling ponds of blackness and heat. Even from where he was, he could smell the sharp, bitter smell of the tar.

There were people there, working in lines. Sartes could see the chains connecting them in pairs as they dredged the tar with buckets and collected it so that others could use it. He could see the guards standing over them with whips, and as Sartes watched, a man collapsed under the beating he was receiving. The guards cut him loose from his chains and kicked him into the nearest tar pit. The tar took a long time to swallow his screams.

Sartes wanted to look away then, but couldn't. He couldn't take his eyes from the horror of it all. From the cages in the open air that were obviously the prisoners' homes. From the guards who treated them as nothing more than animals.

He watched until the cart drew to a halt, and soldiers opened it with weapons in one hand and chains in the other.

"Prisoners out," one called. "Out, or we'll set fire to that cart with you inside, you scum!"

Sartes shuffled out into the light with the others, and now he could take in the full horror of it. The fumes of the place were almost overwhelming. The tar pits around them bubbled in strange, unpredictable combinations. Even as Sartes watched, a patch of ground near one of the pits gave way, tumbling into the tar.

"These are the tar pits," the soldier who'd spoken announced. "Don't bother trying to get used to them. You'll all be dead long before that happens."

The worst part, Sartes suspected as they fitted a manacle to his ankle, was that they might be right.

CHAPTER FIVE

Thanos slid his small boat up the shale of the beach, looking away from the manacles set there below the tide line. He made his way up off the beach, feeling exposed with every step across the gray rock of the place. It would be far too easy to be seen there, and Thanos definitely didn't want to be spotted on a place like this.

He scrambled up a path and stopped, feeling anger join his disgust as he saw what lay along either side of the path. There were devices there, gibbets and spikes, breaking wheels and gallows, all obviously intended to give an unpleasant death to those within. Thanos had heard of the Isle of Prisoners, but even so, the evil of this place made him want to wipe it away.

He kept on up the path, thinking about how it would be for anyone led down there, hemmed in by rocky walls and knowing that only death awaited. Had Ceres really ended up in this place? Just the thought of it was enough to make Thanos's gut clench.

Ahead, Thanos heard shouts, whoops, and cries that sounded almost as much animal as human. There was something about the sound that made him freeze, his body telling him to be ready for violence. He hurried off the path, lifting his head over the level of the rocks that blocked his view.

What he saw beyond made him stare. A man was running, his bare feet leaving bloody smears on the stony ground. He wore clothes that were ripped and torn, one sleeve hanging loose from the shoulder, a great rent at his back showing a wound beneath. He had wild hair and a wilder beard. Only the fact that his torn clothes were silk showed that he hadn't lived wild all his life.

The man chasing him looked, if anything, even wilder, and there was something about him that made Thanos feel like the prey of some great animal just looking at him. He wore a mixture of leathers that looked as though they'd been stolen from a dozen different sources, and had features streaked with mud in a pattern that Thanos suspected was designed to let him blend in with the forest. He held a club and a short dagger, and the whoops he emitted while chasing the other man made Thanos's hair stand on end.

On instinct, Thanos started forward. He couldn't just stand by and watch someone be murdered, even here, where everyone had committed some crime to be sent here. He hurried over the rise, sprinting down to a spot the two would run past. The first of the men dodged around him. The second paused with a sharp-toothed grin.

"Looks like another one to hunt," he said, and lunged at Thanos.

Thanos reacted with the speed of long training, swaying out of the way of the first knife thrust. The club caught him on the shoulder, but he ignored the pain. He swung his fist around sharply, feeling the impact as he connected with the other man's jaw. The wild man fell, unconscious before he hit the ground.

Thanos looked round, and saw the first man staring at him.

"Don't worry," Thanos said, "I won't hurt you. I'm Thanos."

"Herek," the other man said. To Thanos, his voice sounded rusty, as though he hadn't spoken to anyone for a long time. "I—"

Another cry came from back toward the wooded section of the island. This one seemed to be many voices joined together into something that even Thanos found terrifying.

"Quick, this way."

The other man grabbed Thanos's arm, pulling him toward a series of higher rocks. Thanos followed, ducking down into a space that couldn't be seen from the main path, but where they could still watch for signs of danger. Thanos could feel the fear of the other man as they crouched there, and he tried to stay as still as possible.

Thanos wished he'd thought to grab the knife from the man he'd knocked down, but it was too late for that now. Instead, he could only stay there while they waited for the other hunters to descend on the spot where they'd been.

He saw them approach in a group, and no two of them were alike. They all held weapons that had obviously been crafted from whatever had been near to hand, while those who still wore more than the barest scraps of clothing wore an odd mix of obviously stolen things. There were men and women there, looking hungry and dangerous, half-starved and vicious.

Thanos saw one of the women there prod the unconscious man with her foot. He felt a thrill of fear then, because if the man woke, he would be able to tell the others what had happened, and that would set them searching.

Yet he didn't wake, because the woman knelt and cut his throat.

Thanos tensed at that. Beside him, Herek put a hand on his arm.

"The Abandoned have no time for weakness of any kind," he whispered. "They prey on anyone they can, because the ones up at the fortress don't give them anything."

"They're prisoners?" Thanos asked.

"We're all prisoners here," Herek replied. "Even the guards are just prisoners who rose to the top, and who enjoy the cruelty enough to do the Empire's work. Except you're not a prisoner, are you? You don't have the look of someone who's been through the fortress."

"I'm not," Thanos admitted. "This place... it's prisoners doing it to other prisoners?"

The worst part was that he could imagine it. It was the kind of thing the king, his father, might think of. Put prisoners into a kind of hell and then give them the chance to avoid more pain only if they ran it.

"The Abandoned are the worst," Herek said. "If prisoners won't submit, if they're too mad or too stubborn, if they won't work or they fight back too much, they're thrown out here with nothing. The wardens hunt them. Most beg to be brought back."

Thanos didn't want to think about it, but he had to, because Ceres might be here. He kept his eyes on the group of feral prisoners while he continued to whisper to Herek.

"I'm looking for someone," Thanos said. "She might have been brought here. Her name is Ceres. She fought in the Stade."

"The princess combatlord," Herek whispered back. "I saw her fight in the Stade. But no, I would have known if she'd been brought here. They liked to parade the new arrivals in front of us, so that they could see what was waiting for them. I would have remembered *her*."

Thanos's heart plunged like a stone thrown into a pool. He'd been so sure that Ceres would be here. He'd put everything he had into getting here, simply because it was the only clue he had to her whereabouts. If she wasn't there... where could he go?

The hope he'd had started to drip away, as surely as the blood from Herek's feet, where the rocks had cut them.

The blood that the Abandoned were staring at even now, following the trail of it...

"Run!" Thanos yelled, urgency overcoming his heartbreak as he dragged Herek with him.

He scrambled over the broken ground of the rocks, heading in the direction of the fortress simply because he guessed it was a direction those following wouldn't want to go. Yet they did follow, and Thanos had to pull Herek along to keep him running.

A spear flashed past his head, and Thanos flinched, but he didn't stop. He dared a glance back, and the lean forms of the prisoners were closing, hunting them as surely as a pack of wolves.

Thanos knew he had to turn and fight, but he had no weapons. At best, he could grab a rock.

Figures in dark leathers and chain shirts rose from the rocks ahead, holding bows. Thanos reacted on instinct, dragging himself and Herek to the ground.

Arrows flew overhead, and Thanos saw the group of feral prisoners fall like cut corn. One turned to run, and an arrow took her in the back.

Thanos stood, as a trio of men walked toward them. The one at their head was silver-haired and angular, putting his bow across his back as he approached and drawing a long knife.

"You are Prince Thanos?" he demanded as he got closer.

In that moment, Thanos knew he'd been betrayed. The smuggling captain had given up his presence, either for gold or because he simply didn't want the trouble.

He forced himself to stand tall. "Yes, I'm Thanos," he said. "And you are?"

"I am Elsius, warden of this place. Once they called me Elsius the Butcher. Elsius the Killer. Now those I kill deserve their fate."

Thanos had heard that name. It had been a name that the children he'd grown up with had used to try to frighten one another, that of a nobleman who had killed and killed until even the Empire had thought of him as too evil to allow to stay free. They'd made up stories of the things he'd done to those he caught. At least, Thanos had hoped they'd been made up.

"Are you going to try to kill me now?"

Thanos tried to sound defiant, even though he had no weapons.

"Oh no, my prince, we have much better plans for you. Your companion, though…"

Thanos saw Herek try to stand, but he wasn't quick enough. The leader stepped forward and stabbed with brisk efficiency, the blade sliding in and out of the other man again and again. He held Herek up, as though to stop him dying before he was ready.

Finally, he let the prisoner's corpse fall. When he turned to Thanos, his face was a rictus that had almost nothing human about it.

"How does it feel, Prince Thanos," he asked, "to become a prisoner?"

CHAPTER SIX

Lucious had come to love the smell of burning homes. There was something soothing about it, something that built excitement in him too at the prospect of everything that was to come.

"Wait for them," he said, from his perch atop a grand charger.

Around him, his men were spread out to surround the houses they were burning. They were barely houses, really, just peasant hovels so poor that it wouldn't even be worth looting them. Perhaps they'd sift through the ashes later.

For now, though, there was fun to be had.

Lucious saw a flicker of movement as the first people ran screaming from their homes. He pointed one gauntleted hand, the sunlight catching on the gold of his armor.

"There!"

He heeled his horse into a run, lifting a spear and throwing it down at one of the running figures. Beside him, his men caught up with men and women, hacking and killing, only occasionally letting them live when it seemed obvious that they would fetch more in the slave markets.

There was, Lucious had found, an art to burning out a village. It was important not to just rush in blindly and set light to everything. That was what amateurs did. Rush in without preparation, and people just ran. Burn things in the wrong order, and there was the possibility that valuables would be left behind. Leave too many escape routes, and the slave lines would be shorter than they should be.

The key was preparation. He'd had his men arrange themselves in a cordon outside the village well before he'd ridden in wearing his oh so visible armor. Some of the peasants had run just at the sight of it, and Lucious had enjoyed that. It was good to be feared. It was right that he should be.

They were on the next stage now, where they burned some of the least valuable homes. From the top, of course, flinging torches into the thatch. People couldn't run if you fired their hiding places at ground level, and if they didn't run, there was no entertainment.

Later, there would be more traditional looting, followed by torture for those with suspected rebel sympathies, or who might simply be hiding valuables. And then the executions, of course. Lucious smiled at that thought. Normally, he just made examples. Today though, he was going to be more... extensive.

He found himself thinking of Stephania as he rode through the village, unsheathing his sword to hack left and right. Normally, he wouldn't have reacted well to anyone rejecting him the way she had. If any of the young women of this village tried, Lucious would probably have them flayed alive, rather than simply sending them to the slave pits.

Stephania was different, though. It wasn't just that she was beautiful and elegant. When he'd thought that was all she was, he'd thought nothing of the idea of simply bringing her to heel like some glorious pet.

Now that she'd turned out to be more than that, Lucious found his feelings changing, becoming more. She wasn't just the perfect ornament for a future king; she was someone who understood the way the world worked, and who was prepared to scheme to get what she wanted.

That was a big part of why Lucious had decided to let her go; he was enjoying the game between them too much. He'd had her backed into a corner, and she'd been willing to bring him down along with her. He wondered what move she'd make next.

He was brought from his thoughts by the sight of two of his men holding a family at sword point: a fat man, an older woman, and three children.

"Why are they still breathing?" Lucious asked.

"Your highness," the man begged, "please. My family have always been the most loyal subjects of your father. We have nothing to do with the rebellion."

"So you're saying that I'm mistaken?" Lucious asked.

"We are loyal, your highness. Please."

Lucious cocked his head to one side. "Very well, in view of your loyalty, I will be generous. I will permit one of your children to live. I'll even let you choose which one. In fact, I command you to."

"B-but… we can't choose between our children," the man said.

Lucious turned to his men. "You see? Even when I give them commands, they don't obey. Kill them all, and don't waste my time with any more like this. Everyone in this village is either to be killed or put on the slave lines. Don't make me repeat myself."

He rode away toward the sight of more burning buildings while the screams started behind him. It really was turning out to be a beautiful morning.

CHAPTER SEVEN

"Work faster, you lazy whelps!" the guard called, and Sartes winced at the sting of the whip across his back. If he could have, he would have spun and fought the guard, but without a weapon, it was suicide.

Rather than a weapon, he had a bucket. Chained to another prisoner, he was expected to collect the tar and pour it into large barrels to be hauled back up away from the pits, where it might be used to caulk boats and seal roofs, line the smoothest cobbles and waterproof walls. It was hard work, and having to do it chained to someone else only made it harder.

The boy he was chained to wasn't any larger than Sartes was, and looked far thinner. Sartes didn't know his name yet, because the guards punished anyone who talked too much. They probably thought they were plotting revolt, Sartes thought. Looking at some of the men around them, maybe they had a point.

The tar pits were a place where some of the worst people in Delos got sent, and it showed. There were fights over food, and simply over who was toughest, although none of them lasted long. Whenever guards were watching, the men kept their heads down. Those who didn't quickly found themselves beaten or thrown into the tar.

The boy who was currently chained to Sartes didn't seem to fit in with so many of the rest of them. He was stick thin and spindly, looking as though he might break under the effort of hauling tar from the pits. His skin was filthy with it, and covered in burns from where the tar had touched it.

A plume of gas drifted off the pit. Sartes managed to hold his breath, but his companion wasn't so lucky. He started to hack and cough, and Sartes felt the jerk on the chain as he stumbled before he saw him start to fall.

Sartes didn't have to think. He dropped his bucket, lunging forward and hoping that he would be quick enough. He felt his fingers close around the other boy's arm, so thin that Sartes's fingers fit all the way around it like a second shackle.

The boy tumbled toward the tar and Sartes hauled him back from it. Sartes could feel the heat of it there, and almost recoiled as he felt his skin burning. Instead, he kept his grip on the other boy, not letting him go until he'd pulled him safely back to solid ground.

The boy coughed and sputtered, but seemed to be trying to form words.

"It's okay," Sartes assured him. "You're okay. Don't try to speak."

"Thank you," he said. "Help… me… up. The guards—"

"What's going on here?" a guard bellowed, punctuating it with a blow of the lash that made Sartes cry out. "Why are you lazing about here?"

"It was the fumes, sir," Sartes said. "They just overcame him for a moment."

That earned him another blow. Sartes wished that he had a weapon then. Something he could use to fight back, but there was nothing other than his bucket, and there were far too many guards for that. Of course, Ceres would probably have found a way to fight them all with it, and that thought brought a smile to him.

"When I want you to speak, I'll tell you," the soldier said. He kicked the boy Sartes had saved. "Up, you. You can't work, you're no use. You're no use, you can go into the tar like all the rest."

"He can stand," Sartes said, and quickly helped the other boy to do just that. "Look, he's fine. It was just the fumes."

This time, he didn't mind the soldier hitting him, because at least it meant he wasn't hitting the other boy.

"Get back to work then, both of you. You've already wasted too much time."

They went back to collecting the tar, and Sartes did his best to collect as much as he could, because the other boy clearly wasn't strong enough to do much yet.

"I'm Sartes," he whispered over, keeping a watch for the guards.

"Bryant," the other boy whispered back, although he looked nervous as he did it. Sartes heard him coughing again. "Thank you, you saved my life. If I can ever pay you back, I will."

He fell silent as the guards passed by again.

"The fumes are bad," Sartes said, as much to keep him talking as anything.

"They eat your lungs," Bryant replied. "Even some of the guards die."

He said it as though it was normal, but Sartes couldn't see anything normal about it.

Sartes looked at the other boy. "You don't look much like a criminal."

He could see the look of pain that crossed the other boy's face. "My family… Prince Lucious came to our farm and burned it. He killed my parents. He took my sister away. He sent me here for no reason."

25

It was far too familiar a story to Sartes. Lucious was evil. He took any excuse to cause misery. He tore families apart just because he could.

"So why not get justice?" Sartes suggested. He kept scooping tar out from the pit, making sure that no guard would come close.

The other boy looked at him as if he were mad. "How am I meant to do that? I'm just one person."

"The rebellion is far more than one person," Sartes pointed out.

"As if they'd care about what happens to me," Bryant countered. "They don't even know we're here."

"Then we'll have to go to them," Sartes whispered back.

Sartes saw panic cross the other boy's features.

"You can't. If you even talk about escape, the guards will hang us above the tar and lower us into it a little at a time. I've seen it. They'll kill us."

"And what will happen if we stay here?" Sartes demanded. "If you'd been chained to one of the others today, what would have happened?"

Bryant shook his head. "But there are the tar pits, and the guards, and I'm sure there are traps. The other prisoners won't help, either."

"But you're thinking about it now, aren't you?" Sartes said. "Yes, there will be risks, but a risk is better than dying for certain."

"How are we even supposed to do it?" Bryant asked. "They keep us in cages at night, and chain us together all day."

Sartes had an answer for that, at least. "Then we escape together. We find the right moment. Trust me, I know about getting out of bad situations."

He didn't say that this would be worse than anything he'd dealt with before, or let his new friend know just how bad the odds were. He didn't need to scare Bryant any more than he was already, but they did need to go.

If they stayed any longer, he knew, neither one of them would survive.

CHAPTER EIGHT

Thanos felt as tense as an animal about to leap as he walked between the trio of prisoners, back in the direction of the fortress that dominated the island. With every step, he found himself looking for an escape route, yet on open ground, with the bows his captors held, there was none.

"Might as well be sensible," Elsius said behind him. "I won't say that your fate will be any better if you go along with us, but you'll last longer. There's nowhere to run on the island except to the Abandoned, and I'll hunt you down long before that."

"Perhaps I ought to do it and make it quick then," Thanos said, trying to cover up his surprise that the other man had read his intentions so easily. "An arrow to the back can't be that bad."

"Not worse than a sword thrust," Elsius said. "Oh yes, we heard about that, even here. The guards bring us news when they throw us new people to punish. But believe me, if I hunt you, there will be nothing quick about it. Now, keep walking, prisoner."

Thanos did so, but he knew he couldn't make it all the way to the fortress part of the island. If he did that, he would never see daylight again. The best time to escape was always early, while you still had strength. So Thanos kept looking around, trying to gauge the terrain, and his moment.

"It won't work," Elsius said. "I know men. I know what they will do. It's amazing what you learn about them while you're cutting them. You see their real souls then, I think."

"You know what I think?" Thanos asked.

"Do tell me. I'm sure the insult will bring joy to my day. And pain to yours."

"I think that you're a coward," Thanos said. "I heard about your crimes. A few murders of people not able to fight back. A little time running a gang of bandits who did your fighting for you. You're pathetic."

Thanos heard the laughter behind him.

"Oh, is that the best you can do?" Elsius said. "I'm offended. What were you trying to do, lure me in close so you could strike? Do you really think I'm that *stupid*? You two, hold him. Prince Thanos, if you move, I'll put an arrow somewhere painful."

Thanos felt the arms of the two guards wrap around his, holding him tightly in place. They were strong men, obviously used to dealing with unruly prisoners. Thanos felt himself spun around to face Elsius, who was holding his bow absolutely level, ready to fire.

Just as Thanos had hoped.

Thanos surged against the guards who held him, then, and he heard Elsius laugh.

"Don't say I didn't warn you."

He heard the twang of the bowstring, but Thanos wasn't working to break free the way they might have expected. Instead, he spun, dragging one of the guards into the path of the arrow, feeling the shock run through the other man as an arrowhead appeared on the far side of his chest.

Thanos felt his grip loosen as the guard clutched at the arrow, and he didn't hesitate. He surged into the other guard, snatching a knife from his belt and shoving him into Elsius. With the two tangled together, he grabbed the bow from the dying guard, snatching as many arrows as he could while he ran.

Thanos zigzagged as he made his way over broken rocks, sprinting for the nearest cover. It probably saved his life that he didn't try to run back in the direction of his boat yet, but instead made for the trees.

"Nothing that way but the Abandoned!" Elsius yelled after him.

Thanos ducked as an arrow whispered past his head. He felt it close enough to ruffle his hair. The killer hunting him was far too good a shot.

Thanos fired back, barely even looking. If he stopped for long enough to aim properly, he had no doubt that he would quickly find himself killed by one of the arrows that flashed past as he ran. Or worse, he might find himself simply injured enough for Elsius to catch up to and drag to the fortified side of the island.

Thanos dove in behind a rock, hearing an arrow skitter off it. He fired again, went to run, then paused, some instinct making him wait as an arrow flashed past.

Now he ran, sprinting for the trees. He tried to make his run unpredictable, but mostly, he focused on speed. The quicker he could get to the cover of the trees, the better. He fired another arrow without looking, sidestepped on instinct as another arrow missed him, then threw himself behind the nearest of the trees just as a shaft pierced its trunk.

Thanos paused for a moment, listening. Over the beating of his heart, he could hear Elsius issuing orders.

"Go and get more wardens," he commanded. "I will continue to hunt our prince myself."

Thanos started to creep through the trees. He knew he had to cover ground now before more of the armored guards came. Enough of them, and they would easily be able to surround him.

Then he wouldn't be able to get away, no matter how well he fought.

Yet he still had to be careful. He could hear Elsius somewhere behind him, in the rustle of branches and the occasional breaking of twigs. The older man still had his bow, and he'd already proved just how willing he was to use it.

"I know you can hear me," Elsius said behind him. His tone was conversational, as though it were the most normal thing in the world to talk like that to a man he was trying to kill. "You'll have hunted, of course, being a prince."

Thanos didn't reply.

"Oh, I know," Elsius said. "You don't want to give away your position. You want to stay perfectly hidden, and hope you can stay ahead of me. The people I used to stalk out in the world used to try that. It didn't work for them either."

An arrow came out of the trees, barely missing Thanos as he ducked. He fired back, then set off running through the trees.

"That's more like it," Elsius replied. "Make sure the Abandoned don't catch you. Me, they fear. You... you're just prey."

Thanos ignored him and ran on, taking twists and turns at random until he was sure he'd put enough distance between him and his pursuer.

He paused. He couldn't hear Elsius anymore. He could, however, hear the sound of someone cursing to themselves, half angry, half sobbing. He made his way forward carefully, not trusting it. Not trusting anything out here.

He came to the edge of a small clearing. In it, to his shock, a woman dangled upside down by her ankle, caught in a snare. Her dark hair was tied in a braid that dangled down below her, brushing the floor. She wore the rough breeches and tunic of a sailor, tied with a sash. She was certainly cursing like a sailor while she tried to disentangle herself from the rope that held her, without any discernible success.

Every instinct Thanos had said that this was part of some bigger trap. Either this was a deliberate ploy to slow him down, or at the very least, the woman's swearing would quickly bring the Abandoned.

Yet he couldn't just leave her like that. Thanos stepped out into the clearing, hefting the knife he held.

"Who are you?" the woman demanded. "Stay back, you goat-bothering Abandoned scum! If I had my sword—"

"You might want to be quiet before you attract every prisoner here," Thanos said as he cut her down from the snare. "I'm Thanos."

"Felene," the woman replied. "What are you doing out here, Thanos?"

"Running from men who want to kill me, trying to get back to my boat," Thanos said. An idea struck him, and he started to reset the snare.

"You have a boat?" Felene said. Thanos noticed that she kept her distance. "A way off this gods-forsaken rock? Looks like I'm coming with you then."

Thanos shook his head. "You might not want to stay near me. The people chasing me will be here soon."

"Can't be any worse than what I've been dealing with here so far."

Again, Thanos shook his head. "I'm sorry, but I don't know you. You could be on this island for anything. For all I know, you'll stab me in the back as soon as I give you the chance."

The woman looked as though she might argue, but a sound from the trees made her look up like a startled deer and she sprinted deeper into the forest.

Thanos took his cue from her, slipping back into the trees. He saw Elsius come out into the clearing, bow drawn. Thanos reached for the one he'd taken, and realized that he had no arrows left. Without any better options, he stepped out from the tree he was hiding behind.

"I thought you'd be better prey than this," Elsius said.

"Come closer, and you'll find out just how dangerous I can be," Thanos replied.

"Oh, that's not how this works," Elsius replied, but he took a step forward anyway.

Thanos heard the snap as the snare caught, and watched Elsius yanked upwards. Arrows tumbled down from his quiver. Thanos snatched them up and set off back into the trees. Already he could hear the sounds of others approaching; Abandoned or wardens, it didn't matter.

Thanos hurried through the trees, able to head for his boat now that he wasn't being followed. He thought he caught glimpses of figures through the foliage, and behind him, Thanos heard a cry that could only have been Elsius.

One of the Abandoned burst from the trees near Thanos, lunging forward. Thanos should have known that he couldn't hope to avoid them all. The man swung an axe that seemed to have been made from the leg bone of a dead enemy. Thanos stepped inside the swing and stabbed him, shoving him away and continuing to run.

He could hear more of them now, hunting cries coming through the trees. He burst out onto open ground and saw a group of Elsius's wardens approaching from the other direction. Thanos's heart hammered as, behind him, at least a dozen figures in piecemeal armor burst from the trees. Thanos cut to the right, dodged past a charging figure, and kept running as the two groups crashed into one another.

Some kept chasing, but Thanos saw more of them fall to fighting amongst themselves. He saw the Abandoned crash into the wardens in a wave and break against them. They had the ferocity, but those from the fortified side of the island had real armor and better weapons. Thanos doubted that they had any chance of winning, and he wasn't sure he would want them to.

He darted around the rocks of the island, trying to find his way back toward his boat. If he could make it there... well, it would be difficult, when the smugglers had betrayed him, but he would find a way off the island.

The difficult part was trying to find his way. If he'd run straight back along the route he'd first taken, retracing his steps, it would have been easy to find, but there would have been no way to evade the men hunting him. Thanos didn't dare to stop completely either, even though the sounds of pursuit behind him had given way to sounds of battle.

He thought he recognized the beginnings of the path down to the beach, and hurried down it, keeping his eyes open for potential ambushers. There didn't seem to be anyone there. Just a little further, and he'd be back to his boat, he'd be able to—

He rounded the corner to the beach and stopped. One of the Abandoned was there, massive and muscled. He was standing over Thanos's boat, or at least, over what remained of it. Even as Thanos watched, the prisoner struck it with a sword that looked like a matchstick in his hands, shattering some of the planks that remained.

Thanos's heart fell.

Now there was no way out.

CHAPTER NINE

When Lucious got back to the castle, the executions were still continuing. That was as it should be. He didn't want his men finishing this too quickly. He wanted to be there to enjoy it.

More than that, he wanted Ceres to be there to see it for as long as possible. Lucious made a point of looking up toward her window, where he knew she would be chained in place, forced to look out on the scene there for as long as possible. There was a certain satisfaction in that.

Far more than there was in looking back at the courtyard where the executions were to take place. There, men and women knelt in neat rows, while the executioners moved among them with axes. Even as he watched, he saw one push a man down, lifting the axe high overhead and swinging it in a neat arc that left a head rolling along the ground.

"What is this?" Lucious demanded, his voice rising in anger. He'd been away an hour or two at most. Already, though, it seemed that a whole line of Lord West's men had been killed, practically all of them beheaded.

"We're just doing what you said, your highness," the executioner said. "Executing these men."

"And making a complete mess of it!" Lucious snapped. Or rather, they weren't making *enough* of a mess of it. "Beheading them? I want them to suffer! I want you to be inventive. Didn't I tell you to use every means of execution you could think of?"

"Many of Lord West's men have pointed out that they are noblemen," the executioner explained. "And that as such, they have the right to choose death by the sword or axe instead of—"

Lucious hit him then, his armored hand sinking deep into the man's stomach. The executioner was a big man, but with Lucious hitting him that hard, he still doubled over. Lucious snatched his axe from his hands in a swift movement, then brought it round to slam into the executioner's back. As he fell, screaming, Lucious yanked the weapon out.

"They have no rights beyond the ones I say they do! And even with an axe, you should be able to give them a death that's a thing of horror. Here, let me show you!"

He struck again, then again, hacking down at the executioner until he was certain that all the others there understood what they faced if they didn't obey.

When he was done, Lucious looked around for a suitable target to begin with. Maybe if he gave them an example, these cretins would finally understand what he required of them.

"I want you to make this something people talk about a thousand years from now," he said. "Is that so hard to understand? I want you to make these men last days before they scream their last. I want anyone who hears their child talking about rebelling to cut their throat, because the alternative is so terrible. Now, bring me Lord West. We'll start with him."

The silence that reigned over the courtyard didn't do much for Lucious's mood.

"Don't tell me that you've already beheaded him." Lucious watched as one of the torturers was pushed forward. "Well, what is it?"

"Um… begging your highness's pardon, but the king sent for Lord West. He wanted to speak with him."

Of course he did. His father could never just keep out of the way of his fun. One day, he wouldn't have this kind of problem. One day, he would rule, and there wouldn't be anyone making things difficult. The traitors would all be dead, and the people would understand their place.

As slaves.

Lucious nodded to himself at that thought. The biggest problem with Delos was that it had lost clear divisions. The weak had come to believe that there was a whole graduated set of steps between the lowest serf and the king, and the problem with steps was that they created the impression they could be climbed. Well, Lucious would make it simpler when he was king. Those who were not of the noble class would be the property of the noble class, as it should be. Those who argued would suffer for it.

Which reminded him of the *other* thing he had to do today.

"Begin the executions again," Lucious commanded. "And this time, get it right. If I see any more merciful beheadings, it will be all of you in the gibbets. Do I make myself clear?"

There was a chorus of assent.

"Good. Now, open the gates. Let the common folk see. I have an announcement to make."

The guards did as he commanded, and people poured into the courtyard. Lucious tried not to show his contempt. A day or two ago, and he would have slaughtered these people for daring to come together like this. He would have taken it as evidence that they intended to riot, or revolt, or march on the castle.

Even now, he looked round to ensure he knew where the guards were. Discreetly, of course. He didn't want to suggest to these peasants that he was somehow afraid of them.

"Prince Lucious!" a voice called, and Lucious flinched automatically, his hand going to his sword hilt.

When a girl ran forward with a victor's crown of laurel leaves, he guessed that one of his servants had arranged this. Lucious made himself stand straight as he received it, wishing for a moment that it were the real crown. He was made to rule, after all. Afterwards, he would find who had arranged this moment and punish them for not telling him about it.

Lucious stood before the crowd and tried to hide some of his disgust. Couldn't they have found him a cleaner group of people to address? He supposed, though, that the point was to get his message across to as many as possible, so he ignored that aspect of it.

"People of Delos," he began, and for once, he was glad that his father had made him take lessons in the proper way to speak and stand before a crowd. At the time, he'd thought it was a waste of time. After all, he was a prince, and people had to listen to him. Now, though, he was grateful that his voice carried. "My citizens. My people."

They were, after all, very definitely *his*.

"You have seen the chaos that the rebellion has brought to our city in the last days. They sought allies from the far reaches of our lands to try to crush the rightful governance of the Empire. They brought an army to our very gates. They subverted those men whose honor it would normally have been to fight and die for you: the combatlords."

Lucious heard a few in the crowd make noises of disapproval at that. He guessed that his people had planted loyalists there to show the people how they should react. Maybe he wouldn't have them punished after all.

"Today, the threat from the rebellion has ended. I and my soldiers were able to face and defeat the enemy even as they attempted to enter our great city. The traitors are suffering their fates now, while my men are riding out to destroy the last bastions of this blight upon the Empire."

Lucious brought his fist into his palm sharply. "We have crushed them. My ancestors overthrew the tyranny of the Ancient Ones. They claimed the Empire, and we will keep it. If there are any here who doubt our resolve, look upon the bodies of the traitors we are executing. See your fate if you act against us."

34

Lucious watched them looking around, seeing the men being tortured to death there.

"But I do not mean for this to be an unhappy time. It is a moment for the celebration of our victory. Let our king see the joy that is in your hearts at his rule. We expect to see you in the streets in celebration. We expect to hear your voices raised up in songs that praise the Empire's strength."

Again, those planted in the crowd did their part, shouting out their approval even if the others stayed silent.

"And we will play our part in these celebrations," Lucious went on. "We know that the people of Delos love the Stade. As do I! That is why I intend to put on the greatest event that the Stade has seen in its existence. The combatlords who betrayed us will put on a performance that has never been seen before, fighting to their last breath in honor of the Empire. By the end of this greatest Stade, none will survive!"

Lucious half expected them to be chanting his name when he finished that announcement. Instead, he saw the crowd looking at him with something close to horror, while behind him, the screams of the dying continued.

They would come, though, he knew. They would come.

And fear, well, fear would be more than enough for him—once he was finally the Empire's ruler.

CHAPTER TEN

Ceres threw herself against her chains in frustration as she fought to try to get free of her captivity. Every scream and cry from below was like a fresh dagger thrust through her heart, reminding her of just how helpless she was.

She couldn't help. For almost a day now, men and women had been dying, and she couldn't stop it. They were dying for her and they were dying in more horrible ways than Ceres could imagine. After Lucious's murder of one of the executioners, it seemed almost that they were competing to see which of them could find the cruelest way of killing the rebels.

Below, the guards were lowering one of Lord West's men into a boiling vat while he screamed and fought to get away. Ceres would have looked away if she could, but the chains held her in place. More than that, she didn't feel as though she deserved to look away. She had brought the man to this. She had been the one to convince Lord West and his men to come to Delos. She had been the one leading the charge down to the invitingly open gate.

It was her fault, and having to watch them die was her penance.

Desperately, Ceres reached for the powers that she knew lay within her. That she hoped were there, anyway. She'd sought them out so many times now, spending every last hint of energy she had trying to dredge up some response from the power there, but it seemed further away than ever.

Outside, the soldier's screams stopped, and Ceres sagged in place, feeling the chains bite into her wrists. She wished that were an end to it, or even a chance to rest, but there always seemed to be more screams, more torture, more death.

She was still hanging there when the guards came for her; half a dozen of them, all strong men. It seemed that even if she couldn't find the powers that came from her Ancient One blood, the Empire was taking no chances.

"What are you doing?" Ceres demanded. "Where are you taking me?"

They didn't answer. Instead, they took her chains, making her walk between them, pulling on the chains to lead her the way they might have led some dangerous animal. Ceres found herself remembering the omnicat she'd killed in the Stade, what seemed like a lifetime ago. Had they led it in there like this?

They didn't take her to the Stade though. Instead, they pulled her through the castle, and people sprang back out of Ceres's way as though afraid of what she might do, even chained like that.

They brought her to a set of rooms whose opulence only showed the emptiness of her own cell. They were a place of light and gold leaf, elegantly carved ivory furniture and silk drapes.

There was an open door at one end, leading out onto a balcony. As the guards pulled Ceres out onto it, she saw two things: she saw that the balcony had a view out over the courtyard, so that even now she couldn't escape the sight of the executions, and she saw the balcony's other occupant.

Stephania.

Ceres felt anger well at the sight of her. Stephania might not be Lucious, but she was near enough. Every time they'd met, Stephania had tried to hurt her. Ceres surged forward, and found herself held in place only through the efforts of the guards. They fixed her chains to the stone railings of the balcony, holding Ceres back so that she could do little more than stare. She was as helpless as she'd been in her cell.

"My, you do look ragged, don't you?" Stephania said. She, of course, looked flawless. Ceres suspected that she'd probably spent extra time preparing for this meeting, because she didn't have so much as a hair out of place. She dripped with gold and jewels, while deep blue silks accented the coolness of her eyes. "A filthy animal, dragged in from the streets."

"What do you want, Stephania?" Ceres asked.

Stephania signaled, and Ceres's skull rang as one of the guards struck her with the flat of his hand.

"You still don't know how to speak to your betters," Stephania said.

"Should I be grateful that you've decided to take on my education?" Ceres countered. She waited for the next blow to fall, but to her surprise, Stephania raised a hand to stop it.

"We don't want her marked too badly," Stephania said. "We're only borrowing her from Lucious, after all."

Ceres forced herself to smile. "Is that why you're not throwing me over the edge of this balcony?"

She saw Stephania's eyes harden. "You really think I would let things end that simply for you? By the time this is done, you're going to want to throw yourself off there, just to make it end."

"You think I haven't suffered?" Ceres asked. "You sent me to the Isle of Prisoners!"

"And everything would have been so much better if you'd just stayed there, rather than coming back." Stephania sat by a small table, sipping from a steaming bowl. "But you have, and now the rumors are telling me that you claim to have the blood of the Ancient Ones. Oh, don't look surprised. I still hear things."

"I don't claim to have their blood," Ceres said, looking over at Stephania in defiance. "I have it."

Stephania spun the bowl she was drinking from between her hands. Almost casually, she threw it at Ceres. Ceres felt the hot liquid spill down her features as the bowl struck her. She heard the pottery shatter as it hit the floor. On instinct, Ceres fell to one knee, clutching at the spot where it had struck her. Her other hand went down, quietly palming one of the shards.

She saw Stephania step forward.

"Look at you," she said, advancing with each word. "You're pathetic. I don't know why I ever worried about you. Blood of the Ancients? Your blood is what it has always been." Her finger jabbed into Ceres's chest. "That of a coarse, ugly peasant."

Ceres lunged then, using the little slack that was in her chains to get behind Stephania, pressing the shard to her throat.

She felt the tension there in Stephania in that moment, still, but only still because she was holding herself there. She had the tension of a strung bow, or a deer ready to bolt.

Ahead of her, she saw the guards spread out, obviously trying to find a way to help. Ceres kept Stephania between her and them.

"Put it down, or they'll kill you," Stephania said.

"I can still rid the world of you," Ceres said. "If I'm going to die anyway, why not?"

"Because…" She heard Stephania gasp the words out. "Because you'd be killing Thanos's child!"

Ceres let go of her out of pure shock, and Stephania leapt away from her, rubbing her throat. Ceres could see a line of blood there where the sharp edge of the shard had scratched her.

The guards rushed forward then, grabbing for her, one striking her in the stomach. From her knees, Ceres looked up at Stephania.

"No," Ceres said. "You're lying."

"You didn't hear the news then?" Stephania snapped back. "Of course you didn't. A little fool like you doesn't care about the important things."

"What news?" Ceres demanded. "That you're a liar? I knew that already."

She saw Stephania smile broadly. "That Thanos and I are married."

Ceres wasn't sure that any words could have hurt her more. She stood there, and an answer wouldn't come. She couldn't think of anything to say. She couldn't believe that it was true. Finally, she found the breath to speak.

"No," she said. "It's a lie. Thanos would never do that!"

"Really?" Stephania countered. "Ask any of the servants here. Ask anyone you like. I'll summon them. Call it to any of the guards. It was the biggest event of the season. They were all there."

Ceres tried to think of a way that it could still be a lie, but there wasn't one. If it were a lie, Stephania would have tried to control this. Even so, it was almost impossible to believe.

"Thanos would never have married you," she said. "Not unless someone forced him."

"Not only did he marry me," Stephania said, "he was the one who asked me. With you gone, we were very happy. *He* was happy."

"Then where is he?" Ceres countered. "Bring him here. Have him tell me this."

Anger flashed across Stephania's features then. "He's gone, thanks to you. Thanks to everything you set in motion. He had to leave, and if you had just had the grace to stay dead, to not bring... *this* down on the city, then he would still have been here with me and our child."

Ceres almost, *almost* felt a moment of pity for Stephania then, but the hardness of Stephania's expression quickly changed that.

"That's why you're going to pay," Stephania said. Ceres saw her glance down at the courtyard. "Oh look, I believe they've reached someone you care about. Look, go on." She raised her voice. "*Look*, or I'll have the guards force you to."

Ceres stood and looked. What she saw there made her heart break. Anka was still strapped to the post where she'd been at the start. It was obvious that the stress of standing there tied for so long was agony.

And now one of the executioners was approaching her.

He had a long length of wood, and Ceres couldn't work out what he was planning to do until the moment when he fitted it into the rope holding Anka to the post by her throat.

"No," Ceres said.

"Yes," Stephania replied.

"You—"

"This is nothing to do with me," Stephania said. "This is Lucious, but occasionally, he does have his uses. Do you know that *he* asked to marry me? Oh, I won't be saying yes, but it's nice to know how he thinks, isn't it?"

She was babbling on as if this were just a pleasant conversation, rather than a precursor to one of Ceres's friends being killed.

Meanwhile, the executioner was starting to twist the wooden lever, turning the rope, pulling it tighter. He did it as though it was nothing, without a flicker of expression.

"Stop this," Ceres begged. "Stop this. I'll do anything."

"There's nothing you could do that I would want," Stephania said.

Below, Ceres saw Anka trying to struggle against her bonds. Once more, Ceres tried to summon her powers. Surely for this, for her friend... but no, there was no sign of the strength or energy that had been there before.

"Besides," Stephania said, "as I said, this is down to Lucious. We're nothing but observers. I must admit, I was a little put off by the screaming at first, but when it occurred to me that you would be suffering, I got over it."

Ceres threw herself in Stephania's direction, but the noblewoman had placed herself deliberately out of reach. All Ceres could do was stand there and watch while Anka fought for breath, then kicked, trying to get away.

She went still, and Ceres collapsed against the balcony railing.

She couldn't breathe right then. Ceres felt as though the world had stopped spinning; as though none of it made sense. It shouldn't be that easy to lose someone. Guilt and sorrow fought inside her, each trying to find space in which to fill her. Ceres had been the one to talk them into rising up like that, after all. If she hadn't...

But there was no taking it back. Anka was gone. Just like that, one of the few people she'd been able to call a friend was dead, taken from her as if it didn't even matter. She'd been so vibrant, so important to the rebellion, and the Empire had killed her. Lucious had killed her.

And Stephania had stood by to let it happen.

"I'll kill you," Ceres promised. "Whatever else happens, I'll kill you for this."

"And leave Thanos distraught?" Stephania countered. "You wouldn't do that."

She would, though. Looking down at the still form of Anka below, she would. The worst part was that the executioner just left her there, abandoning her while he moved on to another member of the rebellion. To him, killing someone as special as Anka was nothing more than a function to be performed.

Somewhere in it, Stephania called the guards who'd brought Ceres there. Ceres didn't even notice her do it. She was too busy staring down at the scene below.

"I'll say this," Stephania said. "Lucious may be a mindless thug, but when it comes to making people suffer, he does have his uses."

The guards took hold of Ceres's chains, dragging her to her feet like some kind of marionette.

"Just kill me," Ceres said. "Just... end it."

"Oh, not yet, I think," Stephania replied, and Ceres could hear the malice there behind the sweetness. "For one thing, I'm sure Lucious has all *kinds* of things he'll want to do with a prisoner like you, and I'm not inclined to anger him by taking his toys from him. For another..." Stephania's expression hardened. "I want you to suffer. I want you to suffer until there's nothing left of you. Until you can't even remember what it was like to be free, or safe, or happy. After everything you've done, you deserve it."

She signaled, and Ceres felt the guards start to drag her to the door. If she could have broken free then, she would have, either to kill Stephania or kill herself, she didn't know which. Maybe both, grabbing her and throwing them from the balcony together in some kind of final fall.

It didn't matter. Seeing Anka die like that seemed to have drained the last dregs of strength from her, so that Ceres could barely stand, let alone fight her way free. She felt like dead weight, held up only by the efforts of her captors.

"Oh, there's one last thing," Stephania said, and she made it sound almost like an afterthought. Perhaps, to her, it was. "Your brother."

"Sartes?" Ceres said. "What have you done with him?"

"I was going to do this quietly, just to get rid of the last reminders of you," Stephania went on, as though Ceres hadn't spoken. "With you back, though, it provides another lovely way to hurt you. Your friends are dying, you are imprisoned, Thanos married me, and your brother... well, dear Sartes will soon find himself boiling in tar. Enjoy that thought, Ceres. I know I will."

Filled with despair, Ceres wanted to scream, more than anything.

But she didn't even have the strength for that as they dragged her away, her mouth stuck open in a silent wail of anguish.

CHAPTER ELEVEN

King Claudius forced himself to sit as still as a statue on the throne in his chambers, pushing down the anger, the confusion, the sorrow he felt until he could have been just another of the statues of his ancestors, sitting behind him like judging ghosts.

King Claudius had spent a long time considering where he should hold this audience. His wife had suggested the main throne room, but Athena always did have a flair for the dramatic. Lucious would probably have argued against doing it at all had Claudius bothered asking him, because the boy didn't understand the idea of respecting one's enemies.

But Thanos...

"I will not think of him," King Claudius told himself. "I will *not*."

Willing a thing and achieving it were two different things, though, even for him. One of his tutors had once had him read the work of the philosopher Phelekon, from the early Empire. What had he written?

There are some things that even a king may not rule, and his own heart is first among them.

At the time, Claudius had assumed it was some kind of subtle jibe aimed at him. Now, he understood.

His hands tightened on the arms of the throne as the doors to the room opened. Lord West walked in then, his wrists chained, flanked by a pair of Claudius's personal guard. He looked weary, and far from his best, his gray hair streaked with dirt, his clothes marred by blood. Still, the other man managed a crisp bow.

One of the guards went to push him down to his knees, but Claudius stopped him with a raised hand.

"That is enough. *More* than enough. I told you to bring the Lord of the Northern Coast to me, not to drag him here in chains like some slave. Remove those."

"Your majesty," the other guard said, "he might prove dangerous if—"

"I gave you a command," the king said, letting his tone become like ice. "Remove the manacles, and then leave us. See that we are not disturbed. By *anyone*. If you have to hold back my son himself, you will do it."

Now, the guards rushed to obey. That was the point of strength. Of being feared. King Claudius watched Lord West stand impassively as the men removed his chains. Even defeated, even at

42

his age, he stood with the upright bearing of a soldier until the men left, closing the door behind them.

Claudius gestured to a chair he'd had set near the throne. It was smaller and lower, but it was still graceful. Still comfortable. There was a table between the two, with a decanter on it and two goblets.

"Sit down," he said. "I think we have a lot to talk about."

"Is that a command, my king?" Lord West asked, still standing stiffly.

"A request," Claudius replied. "The events of the last days suggest that you don't take royal commands all that seriously anymore." When Lord West still hesitated, Claudius sighed. "Damn it, sit down, West. You're making my neck ache staring up at you, and if I have to stand, I suspect my knees will be worse. Pour wine while you're at it. I know I need it."

That, at least, got a smile from the other man. He sat, and Claudius waited while he poured. He couldn't help noticing that Lord West had as many lines on his hands as his own did.

He hesitated, a pit in his throat.

Then, finally, he said it.

"You know I can't let you live," Claudius said.

His words hung in the air, echoing in the chamber.

It was a hard thing to have to say to a friend like this, even with all the deaths he'd ordered over the course of his rule. Better to get it out of the way. Have done with it quickly.

Lord West nodded, solemn, noble, resigned.

"I know. I knew what it meant when I agreed to attack Delos."

Claudius nodded.

"And yet you still did it."

"I still did it," West agreed.

He didn't seem to want to offer more than that. Couldn't the man open up just for once? Claudius found himself sitting there, not wanting to get this over with now. There were so many things that only his old friend would understand.

"When did we get old, West?" Claudius asked.

"I believe it's an ongoing process," Lord West replied. "The part I find difficult is the division between what my head tells me I should be able to do and what my body can keep up with."

Claudius nodded. He understood that as well as anyone. "I look in mirrors sometimes and I wonder who that old man is there. In my head, I'm still a twenty-year-old, dashing about the outer reaches of the Empire, fighting off Kauthli raiders."

"And falling off his horse," Lord West said.

"We said we were never going to mention that again," Claudius pointed out, but he laughed along with the other man, because even the embarrassing memories were good ones. They were reminders of what felt like a simpler time. "To be honest, I'm surprised that you feel the same way. Even then, I had the impression that you were secretly middle-aged, and you were just waiting for your body to catch up. You were always so serious."

Lord West quirked an eyebrow. "By which, of course, you mean that I was the one sober enough to get us back to our tents by morning occasionally."

"That too," Claudius admitted. How many times had it happened? More than enough that it blended together in memories of West guiding him, and occasionally just carrying him. He nodded to West's wine. "You haven't drunk yet."

Surely his old friend didn't think that he would poison him?

"I'm waiting for you," West said. "Unless he is a food taster, a man does not drink before his king, or his host."

"Always so obsessed with the proper way to do things," Claudius said, but took a sip of his wine anyway. "Better?"

"Much," West said. Claudius watched while he took in the scent of his wine, then drank deeply. "Elphrim Red. Very *good* Elphrim Red. That brings back memories."

"Mostly of you holding up our entire battalion while those dancing priests completed their ceremony to let us onto the salt plain without a 'curse,'" Claudius replied. "That almost cost us the bandits we were chasing."

The image was still as clear as the day it had happened. Why did the past always seem so much brighter than the present, these days?

"Almost, but not quite," West replied. "I knew you'd push us fast enough, and we couldn't afford to offend the nomads there. Besides, it was the right way to do things. One doesn't dishonor a strange land's priests, or their gods."

"I swear, if the Ancient Ones were around today, they'd build a monument on that honor of yours and know it wouldn't fall."

"There was a time they could have said the same for you, old friend," West countered.

King Claudius's grip tightened on his goblet for a moment as he digested the insult hidden within that compliment. What made it sting more was the thought that it might be true. "That isn't the way I remember it. I was the pragmatic one. You were the one who held us all back from doing the wrong thing."

"Pragmatic?" This time, Lord West's laugh was louder. "You were a dreamer. A hot-blooded knight errant who'd read all the stories of the great heroes and who wanted to reenact every one. We spent two weeks chasing around the cloud valleys with Baryn and his squire after some sheep herder's daughter who went missing, got ourselves soaked to the bone because you'd heard too many stories about princesses stolen by the stone folk back in the old times."

For a moment, Claudius didn't remember, then it came to him, all in a rush. He could even feel the rain if he thought about it. "It turned out that she'd run off with some farmer's son, didn't it?"

"And *someone* insisted that we give them half the contents of our money pouches for a dowry so that they could go back to face their parents," Lord West reminded him.

He could remember the weight of them in his hand, passing them to a girl who had probably never seen so much money in her life, even though it had only been a pittance to them.

"I'd forgotten," Claudius said. "How could I forget that? Whatever happened to old Baryn, anyway?"

"He died five summers back," West replied. "His heart."

There was a special kind of sorrow that came with hearing about death when you were older, Claudius had found. When you were younger, death was a distant tragedy. When you were older, death was close enough to almost call it a friend. The loss of those one knew brought sadness, but also a sense of one's own movement toward the dark door. It gripped him then, along with the thought of what was coming with West.

"I didn't know that," Claudius said. He sighed again. "Perhaps that is what age is. A steadily realization that you have started to outlive the men who were your friends."

"You'll outlive me too, soon enough," West pointed out, taking another drink.

Claudius frowned slightly.

He let the long, heavy silence fill the room. The silence of mortality. Of inevitability. Of fate.

"There are men who would beg for their lives at this point," Claudius said. "I think that's what some of those around me had in mind. The great Lord of the Northern Coast, reduced to begging for clemency."

"The people around you are idiots," Lord West declared, raising his glass as if he were proposing a toast to it.

"They are if they think you would ever dishonor yourself by begging like that," Claudius agreed, although he didn't raise his glass. Too many of the people around him *were* fools. "Which brings us to the big question, West. Why dishonor yourself like *this*? Why betray your king? You gave your word, and there was a time I would have trusted the world to that."

"I gave my word," Lord West agreed, "but my family also swore things. Bigger, deeper things than even my personal oath. We swore to protect the Northern Coast until the Ancient Ones returned. Serving the Empire was the way to do that, but that changed. My oath to my family's service took precedence."

Claudius drank slowly, taking in the implications of that. If another man had said it, he would have thought they were mad, but West was so serious, and so cautious, that Claudius knew he meant it. "You truly believe that this girl, this *peasant*, is one of the Ancient Ones?"

"She's no peasant," West replied. "And even if she were, there was a time when you wouldn't have used that as a curse. There was a time when you considered a peasant girl as much worth finding as a princess."

"That was a long time ago," Claudius said. Everything seemed to be a long time ago these days. He shook his head. "Things have changed."

"A lot have," West said. "The Empire, for a start. Do you remember the oath *you* took, the night before they crowned you?"

That memory came back as sharp as a knife. "I was drunk."

"You're working on it now."

Even so, the things a man said when he was drunk could hardly be held against him. Could they? "What's your point, West?"

"You swore that you would be a king who protected the people of the Empire. That you would be a man we could all be proud of obeying." Claudius heard the pause before the next words. "Ceres wasn't the only reason I couldn't stand by anymore, Claudius."

"I have only ever done what was necessary," Claudius countered. He'd told it to himself so many times now that it slipped out easily. Ideals had to bend before the real world, for the greater good. "You have ruled lands. You know that there are no easy choices."

Even to himself, the words rang hollow. It was obvious that they didn't carry any weight with his former friend.

"There are hard choices," West agreed. "Sometimes a ruler must be hard, but he must always be fair. What your son has been doing with your blessing has been a long way from fair."

"The people must be taught!" Claudius snapped. "They must know who their rulers are!"

46

Who did West think he was, telling him how to rule? He, who had ruled for so very long?

"There was a time that they knew that," West said. "Do you remember some of the villages we rode through as young men, when they'd chant your name? They didn't do that because someone had forced them to, Claudius. They did it because the brave young king had come to them, because they knew he would protect them. They did it because you'd fought back the local bandits, or insisted that the local lord drive back the remaining creatures of the old times. They did it because you made the world a better place."

"The Empire still does that," Claudius insisted. "We provide order. The Ancient Ones' pets don't bother people. Bandits run from us to join the rebels—"

"Bandits join your army because they know your son will let them loot all they wish," West said. "Do people come out into the streets for your men, or do they hide in their cellars and hope they pass?"

Claudius sat silently then. He'd drunk too much for this, or maybe not enough. The wine certainly had a sour taste in his mouth then. Or maybe it was something else making him feel that way. The past had a way of sneaking up on a man, no matter how much he tried to push it away.

"Think back to the young man you were," West said. "Or better yet, if you say he's still inside you, draw him out. What would he think of what your son has ordered done to my men? Even with the worst bandits, you used to just behead them, do it clean."

Claudius frowned then. "As opposed to what?"

"You don't even know?" West said. "You must be the only person in the city who can't hear the screams. Lucious is torturing noblemen to death in the Empire's name. Which means he's doing it in yours."

"That's my son you're talking about," Claudius said. He did it automatically, rather than out of fatherly instinct. Lucious had worn that as thin as an entrance hall carpet, over the years.

"It is," West agreed. "It's also the next ruler of the Empire. Now *that's* a thought that makes a man want to drink."

Claudius joined him, but only finished half his goblet. He stared at the rest of the wine as though he might see the future in it. But then, the present was giving him more than enough problems. How could he not know what his own son was doing?

"I feel old, West. There was a time I could have drunk you under the table and still kept going."

"Now I *know* your memory's failing you," Lord West said, with a smile that only took a little of the sting out of his previous words. "When did you last see me drunk?"

"I think it was after the victory in Thornport," Claudius said. "As I recall, there was that business with the twins you couldn't tell apart."

It was hard to keep the humor of it when he knew that his old friend would be dead soon.

"Good times," Lord West said. "Whatever happened to those times?"

"Age happened," Claudius said. "Age and the world."

He drank the wine he hadn't been able to finish a moment ago, then rolled the empty goblet in his hands.

"I wish I could let you live," he said. "But I can't. Whatever your reasons, whatever past we have together, you're a traitor to the Empire. You attacked Delos. You would have overthrown me. There are some things that can't be let go."

"I know," Lord West said. "I've known since the start what would happen if I lost. But let it be an honorable death. I've earned that much."

"That much and more," Claudius agreed. He nodded. "My men will take you to the gallows. There will be a sword waiting for you there. I promise you it will be sharp enough that you'll barely feel it."

Lord West nodded. He considered the decanter. "Probably just as well I'm about to lose my head. This much wine and I'd have a truly *awful* hangover. What about my men?"

"I'll see to it," Claudius agreed. "Lucious has gone too far."

Lord West smiled at that. "Do we have time for one last toast?"

Claudius poured out the remainder of the wine. "What did you have in mind?"

Lord West lifted his goblet. "To the men we used to be."

Claudius shook his head. "To honor."

"To honor," Lord West agreed. He drank his wine in one long draught.

Claudius tried to match him, but only got halfway before he sputtered.

"And that's my cue to leave," he heard West say. "While I'm still ahead in the drinking stakes." He performed one last, crisp bow. "Your majesty."

Claudius watched the guards meet his old friend at the door. He gave the necessary orders. Then he sat back with the last of the wine, thinking of Lucious, Thanos, and what his younger self would have done at a time like this.

"To honor," Claudius repeated, drinking the last of the wine.

He could already feel the tears starting to fall, and he couldn't work out if they were for his old friend, for himself, or for the Empire.

CHAPTER TWELVE

Thanos stood there distraught, staring at the wreckage of his boat. The worst-case scenario had happened: he was stranded on the Isle of Prisoners, with no way out.

The prisoner who had destroyed it spun around, madness obvious in his eyes.

"No one escapes!" he yelled. "Never escape!"

Thanos barely heard the words. His one route off the island, his one way to continue his search for Ceres, was gone, taken from him as swiftly as she had been. Thanos stood there staring, barely able to comprehend the senselessness of it. If the prisoner had stolen the boat, he might have believed it. This was just wanton destruction.

The prisoner charged forward with a roar, and Thanos found himself rushing to meet him. They slammed into one another and Thanos half turned, throwing the man down. The prisoner rolled, coming up, and Thanos pressed in, not wanting the other man to have the space to use the sword.

The bigger man tried to lift his weapon and jab down with it. Thanos caught his arm, barely holding it at bay as he stabbed once, then again, with his stolen dagger. For a moment, it seemed as though even that might not be enough to fell him, as the prisoner roared in anger. Thanos stabbed a third time, and this time it seemed to hit something vital. The prisoner gasped, and the strength seemed to go out of him all at once.

Thanos let him fall, and went back to staring at the remains of his boat, feeling the pain, not so much of its loss as of what it represented. The chance to keep going. The chance to maybe find Ceres. All of that seemed gone now, broken into fragments both by the prisoner and by what he'd learned on the island.

"Piracy, murder, brawling, mercenary work against the Empire, a little burglary to make ends meet. Oh, and refusing the wrong nobleman's advances when I stopped in port once. That was the main one, really."

Thanos spun at the words, his knife coming up. To his shock, he saw Felene sitting cross-legged on a rock not far behind him.

"What?" he managed.

He saw her shrug. "You said before that I could be here for anything. Well, that's what I'm here for. More or less. The full list is quite long. You also said that you couldn't trust me at your back. Well, Thanos, a herd of cattle could have trampled over you the last couple of minutes and you wouldn't have noticed. Yet your back remains remarkably knife free."

As if to emphasize the point, she laid a sword across her knees.

"Where did you get that?" Thanos asked.

"Someone," she said with a smile, "started a big fight where there were likely to be weapons left over. Also, add looting to that list from before. Almost forgot that one."

"Why are you following me?" Thanos demanded. "I don't have anything for you. You can see my boat's destroyed."

Felene shrugged. "What if I told you that I know where there might be another boat?"

"Why come for this one, then?" Thanos asked.

"Because *that* one is well guarded. Too well guarded for just me to take. But two of us…"

"You want me to work with a self-confessed criminal?"

"Last I heard, *Prince* Thanos, you were a traitor. Besides, I just want to get off this rock. Don't you?"

It sounded dangerous. It also sounded foolish, trusting someone like this, but Thanos couldn't think of any better options.

"All right."

"Good," Felene said. "Oh, and Thanos? If you try to leave me behind again, I *will* cut your throat."

The feeling of being hunted wouldn't leave Thanos as he and Felene crossed the island. He glanced around every time they passed a boulder, certain that this time the wardens, or the Abandoned, or both, would jump out at them.

"You need to learn to relax," Felene said. "I know when danger's near."

"Is that why I found you upside down in a snare?" Thanos countered.

"Well, no one's perfect. And I had been running from the Abandoned for close on a dozen days. Come on. It should be just up here."

"What should?" Thanos asked, but he got his answer as they walked up a bluff to look over the edge of a small cliff.

There was a cove below, lined with rocks that looked as though they had razor edges. Shale and dark sand gave way to churning waves, but Thanos's heart leapt anyway.

There was a boat there.

It was bigger than Thanos had anticipated. He'd thought there might be a rowing boat like his own. Instead, this was a skiff complete with a small mast. The whole thing tilted over on its side. The difficult part came in the form of the wardens who stood by it, obviously guarding it while they picked it clean. There were half a dozen of them. No wonder Felene hadn't wanted to fight them alone.

"My noble 'patron' told me that there was money to be made bringing the right goods to the island," she said. "Maybe helping someone off too. He made it sound like a rescue mission. He didn't tell me that this lot would be waiting for me."

That sounded far too familiar to Thanos. "Smugglers did the same to me."

He saw Felene nod. "I just hope they haven't taken everything yet. The Empire sends them hardly anything, so they pick apart anything that comes close. I've been trying to find a clean way down for days. There's a path, but there's only so close even I can get without being spotted."

"So we're going to have to fight," Thanos guessed.

He saw Felene nod. "I just hope you're as good with that sword as you look."

He followed her as she started to lead the way down a path he could barely see in the side of the cliff. She picked her way down as nimbly as a mountain goat, while Thanos did his best to keep his balance there. They moved into place behind a boulder, just a short way from the rest of the beach.

"They'll see us once we move into the open," Thanos guessed. He put an arrow into place in his stolen bow.

"I can get closer," Felene assured him. "*If* you're going to back me up?"

Thanos could hear the uncertainty there. For all her apparent confidence, for all the crimes she claimed to have committed so brazenly, it seemed clear that she didn't want to risk being left to fight alone. Thanos could understand that. He'd already been betrayed once on this island.

"Don't worry," Thanos assured her. "I don't betray my friends."

"Oh, we're friends now?" Felene drew her sword. "That's good to know."

Thanos watched as she crept forward, almost silently, on her stomach. Thanos waited with his bow drawn. To his astonishment, Felene managed to creep almost all the way to one of the wardens. Her sword swept round at ankle height, and he fell, screaming.

The others turned then, and Thanos felt a thrill of fear as he realized just how quickly this plan could go wrong. He saw one of the wardens reaching down for a horn at his belt, while another stood over Felene as she started to stand, drawing a light axe.

Thanos only had an instant to choose, but even though he'd only just met the prisoner, there was no choice to make. He loosed his drawn arrow, and it embedded itself deep in the chest of the man standing over Felene.

He dropped the bow then, charging forward while his newfound companion engaged another with her blade. He drew his own sword, slamming into the group of wardens and cutting down the man with the horn. Even as he did it, though, the horn sounded, in a low, sonorous note that carried clearly over the sound of the skirmish.

Thanos cut left and right, parrying a blow from one warden, then thrusting into a second. He ducked under a swing, then cut upwards in a two-handed blow, bringing down another man.

The last man was already dead, with Felene standing over him.

"Looks like you can fight as well as you said you could. Quick, we need to get what we can into the boat and get it sailing. Thanks to that horn you let them blow, everyone hunting us will know where we are."

"Perhaps I should just have let them kill you instead," Thanos suggested, but Felene was already working to throw supplies onto the boat.

Thanos froze as he heard another horn sound somewhere above, then glanced up to see men atop the cliff there.

"Hurry," Felene said. "There's no more time. We need to push."

Thanos threw his weight against the small boat, and for a moment, it didn't move. The sand around it seemed to clamp it as tightly as chains.

"Push harder!" Felene insisted, pushing beside him.

Thanos groaned as he strained to shift the weight, but now he could feel movement. An arrow stuck in the boat, and that was enough to propel him to one last burst of strength. He felt the moment when the boat started to float free of the sand, and saw Felene leap aboard.

More arrows rained down, but even so, Thanos made a grab for more of the supplies on the beach. They couldn't sail far without them, and it would still take the guards time to make it down to the beach. He hauled a water barrel onto his shoulder, then ran for the water, kicking with it in front of him as he swam for the boat. Already, it was further out than he could have expected.

Arrows landed in the water beside him, each cutting through it with barely a splash. All Thanos could do was keep swimming.

Was Felene leaving him behind? Thanos didn't want to believe it, but then, it wasn't as though he knew her. Fear came to him then at the thought of what might happen if she just sailed off, leaving him to the wardens. Given that he'd left her behind looking for his boat, he could even believe it.

Then he saw Felene at the stern of her boat, throwing a rope out to him. Thanos grabbed it gratefully, hauling himself in with his barrel, then clambering up onto the deck.

Arrows continued to rain down, guards rushing to the edge of the water so that they could continue to fire. Thanos grabbed for a box, lifting it in front of Felene just in time for the wood to acquire an arrow. He started to stand, only for her to push him aside as more shafts struck the wood of the deck.

"Thank you," he said, feeling the water drip from him to the deck.

He saw her shrug. "Well, I couldn't let good water go to waste. So, my prince, since you got me off this island, I guess you get to say where we go next. Back home for you?"

Thanos shook his head. If Ceres wasn't here, there was only one way he could help things back home.

"Haylon," he said. "We're going to Haylon."

CHAPTER THIRTEEN

Sartes's world was filled with heat, pain, and hatred in almost equal parts. It closed in until there didn't seem to be anything else left, and he could barely force his body to keep moving.

"Faster, you two!" a guard snapped, striking him with a switch. It had gotten so that Sartes barely even felt the blows anymore, there had been so many of them.

Even so, he struggled to fill his tar bucket faster. Beside him, he saw Bryant do the same, even though the boy he was chained to was almost skeletally thin and weak by now. Sartes didn't know how much longer his new friend could survive there.

He wasn't sure how much longer he could last, either. The tar pits were the worst hell he could imagine, and more. The work there started as soon as light touched the cages where they were kept overnight, crammed together in stinking, violent proximity. It didn't stop until it became too dark to see, with the prisoners forced to pick their way between the tar pits by the light of the guards' lamps.

In between, there was only cruelty and endless work, so much that Sartes could barely believe anyone survived as long as they did there. As young as he was, the guards forced him to carry barrels of hot tar, scoop it up in metal buckets, work until his skin shone with a combination of sweat and cooled tar. Burns covered him now, so that every brush against rock or other people brought pain with it.

He coughed as a blast of fumes came up from the tar, and beside him, he heard Bryant hacking as though his lungs might fall out. When he looked up, there was a guard there again, pockmarked and ready with a whip.

"Won't be long now before you go to the tar," the guard said. "A day or two, if I'm any judge."

He wandered off, laughing to himself, and Sartes couldn't help feeling a flash of hatred at that. No one should take pleasure in that kind of cruelty.

"He's right," Bryant managed between coughs. "I won't survive much longer."

"Then we need to find a way out of here," Sartes whispered back.

"Escape? No, we can't even talk about it. If the guards hear, they'll kill us!"

"And how is that worse than what's going to happen to us anyway?" Sartes demanded. "Bryant, if we stay, we die. If we get caught, we die. So the only thing to do is not get caught."

"That's easy to say," Bryant said. "But they watch the worst criminals here. They're used to people trying to get away. We're watched and chained in the day, so we'd never make it out of here. At night, we're caged, and we couldn't see the tar pits anyway."

Sartes did his best to disguise the sinking feeling that came with the realization that the other boy was right. "We'll think of something," he promised. "We just have to stick together, and—"

"You two!" the pockmarked guard yelled in their direction. "Get over here! I have a job for you."

There was something about the way he said it that made Sartes sure he and Bryant wouldn't like it, but they had no choice. Hobbled together, they made their way over to the guard, who led the way to where a cart stacked with large barrels of tar sat, a driver waiting impatiently with his team of oxen ready to pull.

"There's space for two more barrels," the guard said, "so you two get the joy of filling them and carrying them back. And quickly. If this isn't done within the hour, I'll feed your bones straight to the pits!"

Just one look at the barrels said to Sartes how difficult the task would be. They were big enough that just carrying them to the tar pits empty would be hard work. Carrying them back filled with hot tar would be nearly impossible. It was a job for a quartet of the stronger prisoners, not for two of the weakest.

"He's trying to kill us," Bryant said, paling beside Sartes.

The guard lashed out. "I'll have none of your back talk, boy. Get on with it."

Sure enough, the barrel was heavy enough that it took both of them to carry it over in the direction of the tar pit the guard selected, with the guard grinning all the way as they did it. He hadn't picked the nearest, of course. Instead, he'd picked an out of the way one, with no one to help them. He was enjoying this.

"Get on with it," he yelled when they stopped breathlessly at the edge. "I didn't say you could take a rest."

He struck Sartes then, this blow stinging even through his numbness to it all. Sartes wanted to fight then, but he couldn't, not chained as he was. Instead, he started work, stooping to gather the first of the tar. Bryant hadn't started, though. It looked to Sartes as though the other boy could barely breathe.

"Get to work, I said!" the guard snapped, lashing out at Bryant this time. "Oh, I've had enough of this. It's time for you to go in the tar, boy. We'll see if your friend works any faster when he sees what happens to malingerers."

56

"Leave him alone!" Sartes yelled as the guard advanced on them.

"You don't want to try to tell me what to do," the guard replied, jabbing a finger at Sartes. "Not unless you want to go in too."

Sartes didn't have a reply to that. Worse, he saw an evil smile play across the guard's face.

"I have a better idea," he said. "How about this, boys? One of you is going into the tar pit, and you get to fight to decide who it is. If you won't fight, it's both of you."

Sartes considered his options, trying to think of a way through this.

"Now, you scum!" the guard ordered, and there was no more time.

Sartes sprang at Bryant, wrestling close to him. The guard was too big to argue with. Too tough to take in a fair fight, and he could always summon more. He was armed too, with his whip and a short sword that meant even together, the boys would be no match for him. It seemed as though the only choice was to obey, but Sartes didn't want to hurt his friend.

Bryant might have been thinking the same way, but even so, the smaller, weaker boy still fought. Sartes felt a knee slam into his thigh, a fist strike his stomach. Maybe it was the shock of it, but an idea came to Sartes then.

"Trust me," he whispered to Bryant. "And be ready when the moment comes."

He wrestled the other boy around, using his superior strength and pushing him back. He heard the guard laugh as he stepped back to let the pair keep fighting. That was the best opportunity they were going to get.

Sartes darted around the guard, and with Bryant staying still, their ankle chains quickly wrapped around the man's legs. Sartes leapt up at the big man's back then, clamping a hand across his mouth so that he couldn't cry for help. Sheer momentum brought them all crashing to the ground.

Sartes held on for dear life, even though it cost him an elbow to the ribs, and a head snapped back into his face. The world narrowed to nothing more than trying to hang on, smothering the guard's calls for assistance. He wouldn't be able to do it much longer though. He was just a boy, trying to fight a man. Only the fact that he was focusing on just one thing meant that he'd succeeded this long. If Bryant didn't see the opportunity...

He did. Sartes caught a brief glimpse of the other boy standing there with determination written on his face, and then the guard went slack atop Sartes.

It seemed to take forever to move the weight out from over him, not helped by the entanglement created by the chains. By the time he managed to stand, Sartes was breathing as hard as if he really had just carried that full barrel. He saw Bryant holding the sword, staring down at it as if he didn't know what to do next.

"The guard will have keys," Sartes said. "He was talking about putting only one of us in the tar. That means he has a key. Help me search, Bryant."

The instruction helped, because at least it meant the other boy had something to do besides focus on what he'd just done. Sartes remembered the first time he'd killed someone, and even though he'd been defending himself, it still haunted his dreams.

"It will be all right, Bryant," he assured the other boy while he found the key and undid their chains.

"No it won't," Bryant said. "I killed one of them. I don't even *know* what they do if you kill one of them. No one dares to do it."

"We dared," Sartes said. "Just like we're going to dare to escape from here. Quick, help me cut up his tunic."

"What?" Bryant said. "Why?"

"We need something we can coat in tar. Something big enough that it will cover the mouth of one of the barrels." Sartes tried to think about the confidence Anka showed when she was giving instructions. The confidence Ceres had. "Help me, Bryant. We have a chance, but we don't have long to make this work."

Somehow, Sartes managed to inject enough certainty into his tone that Bryant started to help, cutting cloth and dipping it in tar in spite of anything he might have been feeling. They draped it over the mouth of the barrel. It wasn't perfect, but even so, anyone glancing inside would just see tar, and not anything underneath. Hopefully, it would be enough.

"What do we do with... with him?" Bryant asked, with a look down at the guard's body. "If they find him, then they'll know what we did."

"Then we make sure they don't find him," Sartes replied. It was an effort to move the bulk of the guard by himself, but he didn't want to ask Bryant to do this. He pushed the dead weight of the body toward the tar, shoving it in with a groan of effort. It disappeared with a wet sound of tar closing in.

If it had been anyone else, Sartes would probably have been horrified by what he was doing, but the guard would have thrown them in there alive without a second thought. That gave Sartes another idea.

Carefully, he arranged the manacles that had been around their ankles, sinking the ends into the tar while leaving the middle snagged on a rock by the edge, where anyone might see it. Hopefully, it would be enough to convince watchers that they'd gone into the tar, enough to buy them some time.

"We need to carry the barrel back now," Sartes said. "Hide the sword in there so they won't see it."

It was a risk. Sartes knew that. If anyone suspected them, they would need the sword in order to fight back. Then again, if it came to that, one sword might not be enough. Perhaps nothing would.

"We can do this," Sartes said, trying to reassure Bryant, and possibly himself. "We just have to stay calm."

They hefted the barrel between them. It wasn't as heavy as it would have been when full, but the need to keep from dislodging their covering meant that they carried it far more slowly than they had when going.

The driver watched them heft it onto his cart with a bored eye.

"Get the other one on there," he said. "I don't have all day."

They lifted it up, and Sartes waited until the driver was looking in the other direction before he gestured. He lifted the covering over the barrel, ignoring the pain of the still hot tar. Bryant seemed to understand, clambering inside. Sartes climbed in after him.

It was a tight fit. Two of the larger prisoners couldn't have done this, but Sartes wasn't large, and Bryant was so slender after being worked almost to death that he hardly took up any room at all. Sartes pulled their makeshift covering into place, hoping that it would look the way he'd meant it to.

He waited there, and the silence had a kind of pressure to it that built with every heartbeat. He could just make out the form of Bryant across from him, quivering in the dark. Sartes wanted to reassure him, but they couldn't afford any sound, any movement.

He heard sounds outside, making out the footsteps of the driver, his grumbling and curses as he checked his load.

"Stupid whelps. Didn't even fill the last barrel. I'll see them whipped when I get back. If they're breathing by then."

Sartes saw Bryant tense and he put a hand on the other boy's shoulder to still him. They sat there in the half-dark of the barrel, waiting. Eventually, finally, Sartes heard the snap of a whip, the creak of wood, and then the rumble of cart wheels turning. He felt movement beneath him as the cart came into motion.

The fear didn't pass just because the cart was moving though. At any moment, Sartes expected the cart to stop as the guards started to look for them. Yet it didn't. It kept moving. It rolled on without stopping, for minutes, for longer, until Sartes had to force himself to keep his head down.

He found a crack in the barrel, barely enough to let in light. Looking through it, he thought he saw the countryside passing by.

Eventually, the cart came to a halt, and Sartes heard the sound of the driver talking to his animals.

"Stupid things you are. Still, at least you won't wander off while a man's about his business in the bushes, will you?"

Sartes heard the sound of the cart driver walking away, and he knew this was their chance. He grabbed the sword, then stood up, blinking in the sunlight even as he looked around to make sure that they weren't actually surrounded by guards just waiting for them. Instead, he saw empty countryside, a few trees, and the figure of the cart driver with his back to them.

Sartes leapt forward, into the driver's seat. The oxen were waiting patiently in place, but at a crack of the reins, they rumbled forward. At the sound of it, he saw the driver turn, cursing at them and starting forward. Sartes passed the reins to Bryant, then stood with the sword in his hand, waiting in case the driver caught up. Seeing it, the man seemed to slow, then stopped.

"Whelps! Evil little things! I'll see you dead for this."

Sartes laughed and started to cut the ties that held the barrels in place. One by one, the barrels of tar bounced off, rolling onto the rough dirt track and spilling their contents as they went. Freed of their burden, the oxen surged forward, and the cart sped up.

"We did it," Bryant said. He sounded as though he couldn't believe it. "We're free!"

Sartes felt the exhilaration himself. But he knew this road was still filled with horrors, and he could not rest until he reached Delos, found a safe place—and found his sister.

CHAPTER FOURTEEN

The last time Thanos had sailed into the harbor of Haylon, it had been on one of the Empire's warships. Now he sailed around a skeletal graveyard of them, burnt-out hulks and half-sunken wrecks sticking out of the water almost everywhere he looked like the bones of long dead sea creatures.

"What happened here?" Felene asked. She guided the small boat around the wrecks as smoothly as she'd brought it to Haylon in the first place. The small boat had been faster even than the galleys the Empire had taken there. "Who did this?"

"I did," Thanos said, the pain of that memory still as fresh as when he'd set light to the first ships. If he shut his eyes, he could still see the burning wrecks and hear the screams of the men he'd killed. That those men had been there to butcher the islanders hadn't made it easier.

They drifted closer to the docks. Thanos wasn't surprised to see armed men gathering there in the colors of Akila's rebels. Of course they would watch the water, and if they saw an unfamiliar ship, it was only natural that they would want to meet it. They wouldn't want to risk spies.

"Looks as though we have a reception committee," Felene said. "Drown me in the deep, you take me all the best places. Grab that rope."

Thanos had gotten used to Felene in the time they'd spent on the boat. She was tough, and treated Thanos with a kind of bluff directness that made him feel surprisingly comfortable. It was better than the people at court who bowed and scraped all the time.

Getting used to her also meant that he could see the nerves beneath that.

"It will be fine," Thanos said. "They know me here."

She didn't look convinced. "If you say so."

They pulled their boat up to the docks, and Thanos saw other Empire ships there, far less destroyed than the ones in the harbor. These were ones that didn't burn in Thanos's memory, complete with the screams of the sailors, yet he guessed that he was still responsible. These were obviously General Haven's ships, from the second invasion force.

Thanos felt the bump of the boat against the dock, and leapt ashore to tie the ship in place. He looked up from it to find a ring of drawn weapons facing him. That was one part he hadn't been expecting.

"You can see who I am," he said. "There's no need for weapons. I need to speak with Akila."

"He'll want to speak with you too," one of the rebels said. "And then he'll decide what to do with the two of you."

Felene hopped down beside Thanos. "So, when you say they know you, is this in the same way that the bounty hunters of the marches 'know' me?"

"Things are complicated," Thanos said, thinking back to the time Akila had come to Delos. All that way just to warn him that he didn't trust what Thanos was doing. Maybe it hadn't been such a good idea to come here after all.

He saw Felene glance around at the rebels as though calculating her odds of running. "Just so long as they aren't so complicated I lose my head."

They walked between the rebels up through Haylon, into an open space surrounded by pillars. There were tables there, set out in the sun, and Thanos made out Akila at the heart of it all, talking to people, organizing and issuing instructions, treating the square the way another man might have used a great hall.

"There are people who would have moved into the castle here," Thanos said as he approached.

He saw Akila look up, and expected a brief moment of friendly recognition. Instead, Akila fixed him with a hard look.

"Tyrants have castles," he said. "I wanted a place where anyone could come to me. I thought I told you that you weren't welcome here anymore."

"You told me to do more," Thanos replied. "I did. I did so much that I found myself shipped to the Isle of Prisoners. Lucious outed me as a traitor."

"But you escaped," Akila said, looking down at some of the papers before him. Did they contain information on him, or did Akila simply not want to look at him?

"Stephania gave me a way out," Thanos said. "She hired a boat to take me away from Delos. She was going to come, but Lucious found us, and he told me… things about her I didn't know."

"And this is the captain?" Akila asked, with a pointed glance at Felene.

Thanos shook his head. "No, this is Felene, a prisoner I met on the Isle of Prisoners. I went there anyway, because I thought Ceres might be there."

"The last I heard," Akila said, "Ceres was dead."

That brought a flash of pain to Thanos, because the longer he went without finding her, the greater the chances were that it was true. Wherever he went, there seemed to be only the anguish caused by her absence.

"I thought she might have come here," Thanos said. "Have you heard anything?"

"I hear a lot of things," Akila said. "But none of them have been about Ceres."

Thanos saw him shuffling papers.

"Shall I tell you some of the reports I have?" he asked. "I have reports of General Haven, who's *still* up in the hills, causing trouble. This foolish old man you claim to have sent is causing me more trouble than anyone else could have. I have reports that Lord West and the rebellion joined together to attack Delos, but you're not with them, helping them. I have reports that they were mysteriously betrayed, and are dying one by one as we speak. At the same time, you're here saying that you were on the Isle of Prisoners and that you escaped before you could be sent there. You tell me that the biggest snake of a noble in Delos hired a boat to get you away from there, and you abandoned her, that Lucious caught you and let you go… do you know how crazy your story sounds?"

"The part about the Isle of Prisoners is true at least," Felene said. "I was there. He got me off the island with him."

"But I don't know you either," Akila pointed out. "And even if it is true… what are you doing here, Thanos? It's not just Ceres, is it? What do you want?"

"I wanted to talk to you again," Thanos admitted. "I wanted to try to persuade you to bring your men to Delos. It's all very well succeeding on Haylon, Akila, but what good is it if you let the Empire keep thriving on your doorstep? If you write off everyone else's chance to be free?"

He could understand the other man's reluctance, and even his concerns about Thanos's commitment, but Thanos could also feel that this moment mattered. The Empire was teetering. Another push, and it might fall. Get this right, and they might *all* be free.

"I know you're worried," Thanos said, "but this is our chance. You have the ships. You have the men. Come now, and you will be able to write your own relationship with the Empire as a friend, rather than as the man who stood by to look after himself."

Akila stood there in silence. Finally, though, he shook his head.

"You ask too much, Thanos," he said. "And I told you before that you aren't welcome here. My men will escort you back to your boat, but then you need to leave. I have a rebellion to run."

"A rebellion that isn't willing to fight," Thanos said.

He saw a flash of anger cross Akila's face. "Go, while you can." Akila turned to Felene. "If it's true that you broke free of the Isle of Prisoners, then there is a place for you here if you want it. Thanos's mistakes are not yours to pay for."

"Oh, I have plenty of mistakes of my own," Felene replied. Thanos saw her look around. "And if you're turning away the likes of him, this really isn't a place for those who've done the kind of things *I* have."

They walked back in the direction of the docks.

Thanos was silent for most of it.

"So much for Haylon," Felene said. "So, my prince, where to now?"

Thanos stood there, shocked. He could not believe he had been turned away. He had expected to have been greeted as a hero, and instead he had been treated as a criminal.

And without their help, there was no way to take the Empire. There wasn't anywhere he *could* go. There wasn't anywhere left where he would be safe.

He slowly shook his head and took a deep breath. If they wouldn't help him take Delos, then he would have to take it on his own.

He gave her a hard look, feeling the resolve firm within him.

"Delos," he said, his voice hard. "We'll sail for Delos."

CHAPTER FIFTEEN

Even in her dreams, Ceres could not escape the dead. No matter how much she wanted peace, no matter how much she sought freedom, they plagued her.

She looked about and found herself in Delos, in the middle of the Stade, the sands there all too familiar beneath her feet. Except now the sands were gray ash, and the stone of the stands was the marble of tombstones. Ceres stood in the armor she'd worn as a combatlord, the only shining thing in the arena.

The dead sat there in row upon row, looking down with the silent passivity of those beyond the realm of the living. They opened their mouths, and instead of the cheering of the crowd, Ceres only heard the screams of the dying. Each scream brought memories with it, of men and women dying in battle, of those Lucious had executed.

Ceres recognized faces there. She saw Anka sitting in the royal box, with the marks of the ligature still fresh around her throat. She saw Rexus beside her, who had died what seemed like a lifetime ago. There were so many there, but every face was one that brought a flash of pain to Ceres as she saw them. The sight of Anka staring like that brought tears to her eyes, and those tears only continued to fall with the others there, turning the ash beneath her feet to something like mud.

A figure stepped up in front of Ceres. The Last Breath swung his crescent blades at her, and Ceres barely leapt back in time, skewering him with a sword that already seemed to be slick with blood. He fell, then rose again.

This time, he was a soldier, striking with a broad-headed spear. Ceres sidestepped easily, but cutting him down only meant that he rose with a different face. All the time, the crowd roared its approval with the screams of the dying.

There were more of them now, coming not just one at a time, but in twos and threes. Worse, there were figures there Ceres hadn't killed, not directly. Garrant was there now, with an arrow still sticking from his throat. A member of the rebellion joined him, the ghost in the dream reaching for Ceres.

Ceres didn't want to fight them, not even like this, in a place that couldn't be real. She hesitated, wanting to stop the violence and the pain. That hesitation was all it took as they grabbed her.

Ceres cried out as the dead bore her to the floor of the Stade, the weight of them as they piled atop her feeling as though it was crushing the life from her. Ceres felt as though she couldn't breathe, every effort to expand her lungs stopped by the pressure there on her, but also by the weight of the grief that ran through her, threatening to wash away every vestige of herself.

Ceres found herself looking up toward the royal box, where Anka and Rexus sat in some grim parody of the king and queen.

"Please," Ceres begged. "Help me."

"You didn't help us," Anka replied. "You led me to my death."

It wasn't the real Anka, because Ceres knew she would never have said something like that, yet the pain at the words was real, for one simple reason. She deserved them. Ceres knew it. She deserved every iota of pain they heaped on her.

She wasn't surprised when Anka extended her hand, turning her thumb toward the floor for death.

Ceres had thought that the weight of the dead was crushing before, but now they piled over her in such numbers that they seemed to block out the light. They formed a sky in themselves, holding Ceres in place, stealing the life from her while she struggled.

As quickly as the moment came, it passed. Ceres found herself being lifted up, the dead raising her like a leaf on the wind. Then it was the wind raising her, and Ceres found herself floating up over Delos, seeing the Empire spread out around her like some patchwork blanket of fields and settlements.

She saw more than that. Ceres saw herself on a battlefield, dressed in golden armor. She saw a throne, while voices chanted her name. She saw ordinary people standing there, looking as happy and at peace as Ceres had ever seen anyone.

The scene shifted, and this world was the same, but different. Where the last had been green and gold, this one was made from rainbow colors. Below, she saw creatures that she took to be deer at first, but at second glance had the torsos of humans rising from their bodies. Ceres looked up at the call of a bird, only to find one crossing the sky with a plume of flame following it.

The world beneath her changed again, the color leaching out of it, leaving something gray and dead behind it, with people who moved like sleepwalkers, and guards on every corner. It was a world that seemed more like a prison. Ceres didn't believe that it could be any worse.

Then the world shifted again, and as she saw the blood running through the streets, she realized that it could.

"I don't understand," Ceres said to the sky she floated in. "What's happening? What is all this?"

"They are possibilities."

Ceres recognized her mother's voice instantly. The landscape around Ceres shifted again, and this time she recognized the place where she stood. She'd stood there only a little time ago, on a hill looking out over the ocean, surrounded by towers of elegant stone. In her dream, the towers weren't ruined though. The Isle Beyond the Mists looked vibrant and whole in a way it didn't in real life.

She felt a wave of love and peace as she saw her mother standing there among the buildings. There were others there, moving from tower to house, laughing and dancing in the streets. Ceres couldn't make out their faces, but her mother's was pristine and clear.

She stood there, and Lycine reached out to put her arms around her. Even like this, it was enough to ground her and bring her back to herself. More than that, it was enough to persuade her that at least one aspect of this wasn't a dream.

"What do you mean, possibilities?" Ceres asked.

"You have a destiny, and a role to play," her mother said. "But you still choose how you play it. So much depends on what you do. There are so many ways the world could end up."

Ceres shook her head.

"It's too late," she said. "I've already tried. I already lost. I tried to take Delos, and it all went so wrong. My powers... they weren't there when I needed them. I couldn't *save* people."

"Sometimes you can't," her mother said, and there was the ghost of something more in her tone. "Sometimes, you try to make things better, and there is only pain, but you have to be patient, and you have to trust that eventually you will be able to help."

"How can I do anything?" Ceres insisted. "My powers are gone, mother."

Lycine's smile was gentle. "Not gone, Ceres. Just... strained. Overused. There are limits on all of us. Sometimes limits based on who we are. Sometimes limits based on destiny."

"You mean that my powers wouldn't come because it wasn't part of my destiny?" Ceres demanded.

Her mother shook her head. "It's better not to speculate. Let me look at you. Yes, you're worn thin. It happened to us, sometimes, when we tried too much, and you have only just come into your powers."

Ceres felt her mother's hands as she coaxed the energy from within her. She ran it between her hands as something like shadow, examining it the way someone might have examined a length of cloth for holes or missed stitches.

"Things feel broken right now, but what is broken can be repaired," she said.

"Some things can't be," Ceres replied, thinking of Anka, and all the others who had died.

"That's true," Lycine said, with another of those strange notes of sadness, "but things can still be made better. Remember that this gift protects you, but it is not the only thing you possess."

It didn't feel like enough.

"I'm still not sure I can do this," Ceres said.

"You can," her mother insisted. "Remember that I love you. Remember who you are. If we had time… but there is never enough time. You have to go back, my daughter."

"Back to my chains," Ceres said.

"Back to your destiny. Remember what you saw. What might be if you succeed, and if you fail."

Ceres wanted to say more. She wanted to stay there, both to spend more time with her mother and to put off the moment when she had to find herself in chains again. Already though, the dream was fading. Light was coming in through her cell window, making her blink in the morning sun as she started to wake.

Ceres could hear the sounds of booted feet outside her cell as she hung in her chains. She tried to raise her head to see what was happening, but she barely had enough strength to do it.

She heard the sound of wood slamming into stone as the door opened. Four guards piled into the cell, all with expressions that promised violence, despite the half hoods they wore.

"It's time to die," one said.

"Almost," another added. "We've got a little time first."

"Enough time to make you scream, at least," a third added.

"Enough time to have some fun," the last one said. "Prince Lucious said we needed to kill you, but he didn't say how long to take about it."

The four of them moved forward, and Ceres struggled against the chains that held her. She felt real fear then, not just because of the fact that these men had come there to kill her, but because of everything else they obviously intended.

"Can we cut her before we start?" the first one asked. "I always like it when they're bleeding a little."

"After," the second insisted. "After, we can beat her, whip her… whatever we want."

"Or just cut her throat," the third said.

The second shook his head. "And what will Prince Lucious say when he inspects the corpse and finds no marks on it? No, we do this *thoroughly*."

He reached out for Ceres then, his hand brushing her cheek. Ceres cringed back then, pushing herself back against the wall as if she might be able to push herself through it if she only tried hard enough.

She felt the hands of the others on her, pushing her into place on the wall, holding her there as firmly as the chains, so that she couldn't even begin to move to escape them.

"They say she was Prince Thanos's favorite," one said.

"They're all the same once they're screaming."

Ceres told herself that she wouldn't scream. That she would find a way to fight, even if all that did was make them kill her quicker. Maybe it would even be better that way.

She felt it then: the same feeling that she'd had when her mother was there with her in her dream. The same feeling that she'd had when her mother had run Ceres's energy through her hands as casually as breathing. Ceres felt her mother's presence in that moment, and in the same instant, her power flared into life.

The energy roared up through her, feeling as familiar as a loyal dog coming running after too long outside. It snapped like dark lightning through Ceres's veins, and she felt the strength that came with it, the vitality. In that moment, all the tiredness and the weakness fell away from her.

More than that, it was easy to shape the energy that crackled up through her, easy to send it out almost without thinking about it, arcing through the contact between her and the vilely questing hands of the guards. One moment, Ceres was reeling back beneath their touch, the next, they fell still, so very still.

As still as the stone that now sat in place of their flesh.

Ceres stared at the statues there, their expressions caught, perfectly and permanently, between cruelty and shock. She tried to feel some hint of regret for what she'd just done, but there was nothing there but hate for them.

Ceres summoned her strength to her. Now she had enough to snap the chains that held her, leaving their trailing ends dangling as she shoved the statues away from her. Ceres stood there for a moment, feeling the power rising within her.

She ran.

She didn't know enough about the layout of the castle to be certain about her way out of there, but she could guess. Ceres headed down, and out, heading for the extremities of the castle, trying to avoid servants and guards.

Even so, she started to hear shouting voices behind her.

Ceres kept running, taking turnings at random, reasoning that if even she didn't know where she was going, her pursuers wouldn't. She ran the length of a corridor, coming out onto a small balcony. Below it, a waterway ran in deep, murky silence.

"Wrong way," Ceres said, and turned round, trying to think of a better way to go.

It was too late for that though. There were already guards making their way along the corridor, swords drawn. A part of Ceres wanted to fight, but the truth was that she didn't know if her powers would hold or not. She couldn't take the risk.

There was only one thing she could do.

Carefully, almost delicately, Ceres raised herself onto the edge of the balcony, looking down at the waterway.

I hope that's as deep as it looks.

She jumped.

CHAPTER SIXTEEN

For the first time since setting sail from Delos, Thanos didn't know what to do. Leaving, he'd had a mission: he was going to find Ceres. Then, when she hadn't been on the Isle of Prisoners, it had seemed obvious to go to the rebellion on Haylon.

Now, he drifted, unsure what to do next. The boat was doing the same, with Felene fishing off the bow, apparently happy enough to waste the time with the sail down, drifting close to the small islands near Haylon. While Thanos watched, she pulled up a spiny rainbowfish, apparently unconcerned by everything around them.

Thanos wished things were as easy for him.

"Where to then, oh prince?" Felene asked with a glance back over her shoulder. "Still Delos, or do we just drift until we bump into land?"

"Is that a nautical term?" Thanos asked, but the attempt at humor didn't disguise the indecision behind it. He'd said Delos only because it was his home. He hadn't thought beyond that.

"I could shout 'land ahoy' when we do, if it helps." Felene gutted the fish expertly, and Thanos saw the gulls gathering above the boat. "Seriously, though, do you have a plan that's not going to get us both killed, thrown off an island, or imprisoned?"

Thanos could hear the concern there. He had to admit, he shared some of it. Haylon had been the safest place to go. Delos... well, Delos was anything but safe.

"You didn't have to come with me," Thanos pointed out.

"It's my boat." As if to reinforce the point, she started to raise the sail, putting the boat into motion.

"I could have found another," Thanos said. "Akila would have done that much, at least."

He hoped. After everything the two had gone through together, it was hard to believe how little Akila trusted him now. He'd thought the other man would have seen Thanos's escape from Delos as proof of his commitment, but it hadn't worked out like that. Thanos had gone seeking allies; instead, he was alone, or nearly alone.

"So why did you follow me?" Thanos asked again. "You could have stayed there. You could have set off alone in your ship. You could have gone anywhere, but you chose to come with me."

Felene flashed him a smile. "Does the mighty prince think I'm smitten with him? Sorry to be the bearer of bad news, but you aren't my type."

Thanos wanted to say that he hadn't given it a thought, but he had wondered where this might be heading, given Felene's eagerness to go with him. He had to admit it stung his pride a little too, to be put down so quickly.

"If not that, then what?" Thanos asked, and something must have come through in his tone, because he saw Felene smirk.

"Well, there's the part where I owe you a debt," Felene said, "and I pay my debts. Any debts that aren't to wine merchants or tailors, anyway. And besides, how would I fit in with a well-organized band like that?"

"You're saying I'm disorganized?" Thanos asked.

"I'm saying that it looks as though there are going to be a lot more opportunities for fun and adventure around you than sitting on an island trying to root out some limpet of a general."

Was that really all it took to get the former prisoner to follow him?

"But we'll both be a lot less embarrassed if you don't bring the romance thing up again," Felene suggested. "As I say, you're not my type. *And* you're a married man."

Stephania. Just the thought of her name made Thanos tense, caught between what he'd done and all the things he could have done instead. He could have taken her with him. He could have seen her executed for what she tried to do to him. He could have protected her from Lucious.

He could have, at least, tried to protect his unborn child.

"That's complicated," Thanos said.

"Well, maybe you can take some time to think about it while you get the rest of the sails up?" Felene said, pointing. "We need to get moving, because we have visitors."

Thanos looked in the direction she indicated, and saw a dot that was slowly resolving itself into a ship.

"They've seen us?" Thanos asked.

"They're coming straight forward, so I doubt it's chance," Felene replied.

"Pirates?" he asked.

"More likely imperials cordoning the island. Not people we want to meet in either case." Felene gestured to the ropes. "Don't just stand there, start hauling."

She gave the command as casually as if Thanos were a common sailor.

"Can we outrun them?" Thanos asked.

"Outrun what looks like a galley with two large sails and three banks of oars?" Felene said. "Not a chance. But we can go places they can't. Hold on."

Thanos gripped the boat's rail as she jerked the tiller, then barely ducked in time as the sail jibbed round. The open sea gave way to the sight of land as the boat came to point at the small islands nearby.

"We're going between them?" Thanos asked.

"If you can't run from things, and you can't fight them, might as well try something crazy," Felene said.

"So this is crazy?" Thanos asked. "That's not reassuring, Felene."

"Oh, I'm sure it will be fine," she replied. "I can go shallower and closer to shore than that monstrosity can. Well, probably. And if not, I'll get to yell land ahoy earlier than we thought. Oh, relax. This is a long way from the craziest thing I've done."

That wasn't particularly reassuring either, but there really didn't seem to be any better options. Their small craft skimmed in close to the islands scattered ahead like crumbs from some giant's table, skipping across the waves while Thanos did his best to hold on.

"That rope, haul when I say!" Felene called. "Not before!"

Thanos readied himself, getting a grip and setting his feet into place against the deck. Behind them, the galley was gaining. There was no chance of outrunning them, but the small boat skimmed into a space between sharp-edged rocks, and Thanos saw Felene pulling at the tiller.

"Now!" she called, and Thanos could hear the urgency there.

Thanos pulled on the rope with all the strength he could muster. The roughness of it burned at his hands, but he ignored the pain and kept pulling. He saw the sail furl briefly, the lack of wind momentarily stilling their onward rush. In that stillness, Thanos felt the boat jerk around, navigating a seemingly impossible route between the rocks.

"Don't just stand there staring," Felene yelled. "We're only just getting started. That side, we'll need the ballast. And get that sail up again. We don't want to be in bowshot when they get close."

Thanos threw himself to the other side of the boat, countering the suddenness of the next turn. There was something pure, something clean about simply acting, about not having to think about what came next when he could just react.

"You know my father abandoned us when I was just a girl?" Felene yelled as she pulled the boat into a space so tight Thanos

73

could have reached out to touch the roughness of the rock wall nearest his side.

"Is this really the moment?" Thanos countered.

"Some things are important!" Felene yelled back. "Looking back, it's pretty obvious he was a wastrel drunk, but when you're a child you don't see it. He walked out one day, and I never knew why. I thought it was all my fault. Quick, head down. We're jibbing again."

Thanos ducked as the mast came across, close enough that he thought he could feel it as he passed. This was *not* how he'd expected having this conversation.

"So this is what turned you to a life of crime?" Thanos guessed as they came out into what looked like clear water.

"What?" the former prisoner said with a frown. "No! I did *that* because it was fun! That wasn't my point."

"What was your point then?" Thanos demanded.

Felene looked as though she was going to answer, but the galley chose that moment to round the small islands that they'd darted between. Thanos held his breath as he saw a catapult on the front of the galley, a flaming bundle sitting there ready to throw. If that so much as grazed their boat, it would quickly sink. For the first time in this chase, Thanos finally had enough time to feel fear.

"Through there," Thanos said, pointing to another collection of small islands. The gaps there were wider, but maybe that could be a good thing.

Felene nodded, obviously understand. Thanos felt the boat surge ahead under her guidance.

"So, my point," she said, as if this were all as normal as wandering along a street. "I guess it's that there are things you don't do. I'd have thought you'd know all about them, being a noble."

"You haven't met the same nobles I have," Thanos said.

Behind them, he saw the galley fire. The flaming cargo arced through the air, and for a moment it seemed as though the world held still. Thankfully, their small boat didn't, jinking to the side while the missile sent up a spray of steam as it hit the water.

"I've met a few of them. Simpering girls, all pretty enough in their way, but hardly fun when they think the world revolves around them. Young men who think they get whatever they want, and there are no consequences."

Thanos tensed as they dove into the new hiding space, their boat slipping into a lagoon ringed by sharp boulders.

"I'd have thought you'd have been right alongside that," Thanos said.

Felene didn't answer at first, but instead looked back. Thanos looked with her as the galley tried to close on them. The wider space of the lagoon had obviously convinced its captain that they could chase the small boat in there, yet the rocks beneath the water made that far too treacherous.

The galley dove in after them, but those rocks caught on it like teeth, ripping into it from underneath. Thanos heard the screech of stone on wood as the rocks started to rip their pursuers' ship apart. He saw it tilt unnaturally to one side, the oars backpedaling.

He stood there, watching the damage, watching men running about on the deck, trying to recover from what had just happened. Even as he watched, he knew that they wouldn't. The best that they could hope for now was to make it to the nearest island.

He knew that these would be more deaths on his conscience if they didn't make it. More to add to the tally that had started with Haylon, if not before.

"There are always consequences," Felene said, as she twitched the tiller to send their boat through another gap. "You always end up paying them, even if it's only to yourself. Debts, remember?"

Thanos wasn't sure that he should be taking advice from a self-confessed criminal. He definitely wasn't sure if the middle of a chase like that had been the right time to discuss it. There was only one problem:

Felene had a point.

He had a wife waiting for him back in Delos. A wife he had abandoned when she was carrying his child. Yes, what she had done to him was unforgivable, but his own actions had been those of a coward. He'd chosen not to take her with him. He'd chosen to abandon her with Lucious. He'd let his anger and his disgust get the better of him. He'd abandoned his wife to chase the dream of Ceres.

"From that expression," Felene said, "I guess we're heading back to Delos after all?"

Thanos nodded. "I owe Stephania more than this. Maybe... maybe things can never be as they were, but I can make something work."

"There is the minor problem of you being declared a traitor," Felene pointed out. "Also me being wanted in connection with... well, lots of things. But mostly the traitor thing."

"I'll find a way," Thanos said. "Maybe I can get Stephania out of there."

"I get to travel with a prince *and* a beautiful princess?" Felene said. "How is she at hauling on ropes?"

"She would hate every minute of it," Thanos replied, and as he said it, he knew it wouldn't work like that. Stephania was someone who needed comfort and protection. Yes, she had harder edges to her than Thanos had thought, but they couldn't bring up their child unless they could find somewhere safe to run to.

"Well," Felene suggested, "maybe things have died down. That happens with you nobles. I knew this duchess once, out of one of the principalities beyond the Spine. Exiled from her homeland for some plot or other, hired me to harass its ports. Then everything shifted, some relative died or something, she was coming home to a hero's welcome, and I had to ship out quick."

Thanos shook his head. "I don't think it will be that simple."

There were too many things going on in the Empire for that, and given who his father was, Lucious wouldn't let this go.

"But we're still going back?" Felene said. "Because you're making this sound like a worse plan by the moment."

Thanos paused. He knew Felene was right. He couldn't just wander back into Delos without a plan and expect everything to turn out all right. Felene had said more than that though.

"I have to do this," Thanos said. "And like you said, sometimes crazy is what you need."

"Going back is dangerous," Felene said. "Crazy is... you're not just going back, are you?"

Thanos shook his head. "It's gone beyond that. If I can get Stephania out easily, I will, but they'll have her watched now. So I'll probably have to do things another way."

"What other way?" Felene asked.

"I'll go to the king," Thanos said. "And offer my submission. If he won't accept that, then I'll offer my life for hers. As you said, there are things you don't do, and leaving her behind is one of them."

He felt better for saying it. Now the words were out, it felt real somehow. Definite.

"Not going to try to talk me out of it?" Thanos asked.

He saw Felene shrug.

"The way I see it, the worst-case scenario is that I get to run off with a princess and try to convince her of the joys of the pirate life." She grinned wide. "Besides, I always did love a crazy plan."

CHAPTER SEVENTEEN

King Claudius sat alone, contemplating life. Contemplating death. It was strange how, the older he got, the more those two seemed to be bound up with one another. He sat in his private chambers, his sword bare across his knees, the way it had been when Thanos had come to him. Thinking back on what he'd done to his son then, it was hard to feel anything but shame.

Lord West would be long dead by now. That thought brought the dull ache of sadness with it, because he had been a good man, an honorable one. King Claudius had always seen West as everything a nobleman could hope to live up to. What did that say about him?

He'd been thinking about that for a long time now, sitting in his room, the faces of his ancestors looking back in sculpted stone from their niches.

"Did you ever feel like this?" he wondered aloud. "Did you ever look back on the things you did and realize that you had done more harm than good?"

He couldn't imagine it. Just think of the names of his ancestors. Cleus Ironfist, who crushed the forest lands of the eastern Empire, leaving enemies hanging from every tree, and tearing up so much that farmers grazed their herds there now. Barathon the Bloody, who fought thirty duels himself against those who would challenge him, losing only the last, to the one son he hadn't killed.

"And what will they say about me?" Claudius asked himself. That he was the worst of the lot, perhaps. That in his blood-soaked reign, the Empire tore itself apart so thoroughly it was never the same again. That there was never another ruler as cruel or dishonorable.

Except that wasn't true, was it?

"There is still my son to come," Claudius said to the ghosts of his ancestors. He would make all of them look like nothing.

He stood at the sound of the door opening, and saw the servant who entered shrink back in fear at the sight of him. Perhaps it was the sword, but Claudius doubted it was just that. Even without it, how many times had he seen servants and slaves cringe away? How many times had he summoned serving girls to him, only to feel their fear?

"What is it?" Claudius asked.

"F-forgive me, your majesty, I know you didn't want to be disturbed... it's just—"

"Out with it, man," Claudius snapped on instinct, and the servant actually shrank back against the wall, not saying anything.

Claudius could guess what he'd been doing there, though. He'd been the poor, unfortunate fool low enough down the ladder to be ordered into his chambers even after he'd said no one should come in.

Someone had sent him in to check that the king was still breathing and well. Possibly his wife, or his son, although in truth it was more likely to be one of his guards. Athena and Lucious were both perfectly happy getting on with their own endeavors without him there. Possibly too happy, given what some of those efforts amounted to.

Just the sight of the servant there was enough to tell Claudius what he needed to do. What he should have done years ago.

"Fetch water and a basin," he ordered the man. "Have robes brought, too."

"The gold, your majesty?"

King Claudius shook his head. "Mourning black. No jewels beyond a simple circlet. After all the death, this is not a time for gaudiness. And tell my chamberlain to announce that I will be speaking from my balcony at noon. The people are to be allowed into the streets to listen. The guards are not to strike at them. And bring paper. This needs to be said right."

"Yes, your majesty," the servant said, hurrying away to put the instructions into practice.

King Claudius prepared himself carefully, observing himself in a mirror for what was probably the first time in days, really *looking* at himself for what seemed to be the first time in forever.

The man he saw wasn't the man he'd hoped to see when he was younger. Not that his younger self had ever conceived of the possibility of really becoming old. If he had thought about it, Claudius suspected that he'd envisioned himself as some broad shouldered behemoth of a man, no more than a few gray hairs flecking his beard, as strong as ever and universally loved.

Time showed the truth of these things like nothing else.

Claudius did his best with the clothes he had, summoning a barber to trim his beard back to neatness, trying to blink some of the dark rings from around his eyes. He picked out somber, elegant clothes from those offered to him, and smiled as he realized that he was wearing the sort of thing Lord West usually favored. Perhaps that was appropriate, today, so soon after his old friend's death.

He made other preparations too, writing down his thoughts, trying to get them in order. Ultimately, though, he knew what he needed to say, and to do.

"Your majesty," the servant who'd been brave enough to enter the room said. "It is approaching noon."

Claudius looked out of his windows, and sure enough, the sun was high in the sky. It was time. He just hoped as he stepped out onto his balcony that his people had come out to hear him speak.

They had. Claudius felt a moment of apprehension as he saw the sea of people there. Normally the sight of so many peasants would have brought real fear with it at the prospect of riot, rebellion, or worse. He certainly wouldn't have felt any sense of connection to them or concern for them.

Now, though, he could see how thin and haggard some of them were. He could see children who looked as though they hadn't eaten in days, and for once, he didn't feel the urge to blame their parents' indolence. They hadn't caused this.

"My people," King Claudius said, and for once, he felt it. "The months gone past have been hard ones for you. I know this. The conflict against the rebellion has cost you a lot."

Once, he would have left it there, but he thought of all the things he'd ordered done, and the leniency he'd shown to Lucious over his actions. He saw them staring up silently, expecting another tax, another round of conscriptions, and he kept going.

"*We* have hurt you. We have taken your property to fund our feasts. We have taken your children to fight our wars. We have killed you as if you are enemies to be destroyed, not subjects to be protected. Well, that stops today."

He could feel the change in the crowd below. They were quiet now, listening in something other than fear.

"The time for bloodshed has passed," he said. "We fought the rebellion, but the cost of doing so has been your homes and your lives. We cannot restore the dead, but I promise you that my soldiers will rebuild every house burned, restore every home stolen."

That got a murmur from the crowd, as if they couldn't quite believe what they were hearing. That, more than anything, told Claudius just how necessary this was.

"There will be no more arbitrary seizures of your goods, or of you," the king said. "From now on, the old tithes will be restored, and no more than that will be taken."

That got a sound of approval.

"As for what is left of the rebellion, I have realized that when it comes to our enemies, we have a choice: we can destroy them utterly, or we can make them our friends. The second option always struck me as a sign of weakness, and as a thing that would invite our own destruction. Yet now I believe that it is continuing this pointless war that is tearing us apart. As of today, any rebels who were taken are to be freed, and no vengeance will be sought for the war."

That did get a cheer, and a bigger one than Claudius had heard in a long time. He'd heard cheers after battles and cheers forced from the lips of obedient townsfolk. This, though, was more than that. It was the cheer of a people realizing that a heavy yoke was being taken from around their neck. It was the cheer of a people who had just been told that they were going to be free.

For that to be true, though, at least one more thing had to change.

"With me," he said to his bodyguard. "There is still work to do today."

"Where to, your majesty?" the man asked.

"The hall of scholars," Claudius replied. "Old Cosmas and I need to talk."

It had been a long time since he had made the journey down through the castle towards its library. As a young man, he had read the tomes of every learned scholar, from the tacticians to the philosophers. He had stared at maps of the lands beyond the sea, wondering what it would be like in the deserts of Felldust or the pirate lanes of the Free Cities.

As he'd grown older, responsibilities had gotten in the way. He'd had an empire to rule. There had been no time left for reading, or for the kind of studies Old Cosmas had always wanted to push him into.

It took a while to get down to the hall of scholars. Plenty of time in which Claudius could have reconsidered what he was going to do next, yet every step only made him more certain that it was the right thing to do. Even the cheers of the crowd below said that, echoing as they still did down the corridors of the castle.

"I built one legacy," he said to himself. "I can build another."

"Your majesty?" his bodyguard said.

Claudius shook his head. "It doesn't matter. What's your name, soldier?"

"Krin, your majesty."

"And you've served me how long?"

"Close to ten years, your majesty."

Close to ten years, and Claudius didn't know his name. Yes, there were a lot of things that needed to change.

He reached the doors to the hall of scholars, stepping inside and looking around at the piles of books and scrolls. He spotted Cosmas toward the back, working on what was probably a copy of an original scroll, or perhaps on some fragment of his ongoing work on comparing long dead languages.

"Wait outside," Claudius told Krin. The bodyguard nodded, and went to the door. Still, the royal scholar didn't look up. "Cosmas? *Cosmas.*"

"Hmm... oh, I beg your pardon, your majesty. Have you been there long?"

He wouldn't have accepted it from anyone else, but Cosmas had always been this way. "Not long. Are you working on anything in particular?"

"I found a tract on the pictographs of the valley people of the Lesser Dust," Cosmas replied. "I believe we talked about them once. They have the most fascinating burial customs."

Probably they had spoken about it, at some long forgotten point in the past. It was the kind of thing that Cosmas had a good memory for, while a thousand and one things had happened to Claudius since then.

"But that is not what you've come to me for, I imagine," Cosmas said. Claudius watched while he set aside his stylus. "How may an old scholar help you, your majesty?"

Claudius took a breath. "A long time ago, I came to you and I ordered records erased, lost, reordered. You did as I commanded, but I imagine it must have pained you to do it, Cosmas."

"To follow the instructions of my king?" Cosmas replied. He bowed his head slightly. "Yes, it was... testing to my commitment to knowledge to help hide it."

"You did it anyway, though," Claudius said. Now was the moment. "What if I asked you to undo it?"

"What exactly are you commanding?" Cosmas asked, and Claudius could hear the caution there. Of course he could. This was something he'd forbidden the old man to speak of to anyone.

"I have been thinking a lot since Lord West came to me," he said.

"They say he walked to the block bravely," Cosmas replied.

Claudius shook his head. "Of course he did, but it should never have come to that. I have hidden too much, from myself, and from the world. I wish to acknowledge my son."

He watched the rise of Cosmas's eyebrows. "Your son?"

Claudius could understand the reticence, but this was a time to act, not wait. "Let's not play games, Cosmas. I want you to write Thanos back into the lineage of the Empire, where he belongs. I wish it to be known that he is my son. My firstborn son."

Cosmas drummed his fingers on his desk. "You are aware, your majesty, that this would make him… your heir?"

An act that would come with consequences, no doubt; not least Athena's disapproval. Yet the truth was that all actions had consequences, and those of the actions he'd taken all those years ago had twisted the whole course of the Empire since. With Thanos as his heir, perhaps there would have been no uprising. Perhaps everything would have been different.

"I know what it will mean," Claudius said. "It will mean that everything changes. It will mean that nothing will be the same again. Sometimes, though, things need to change, and things here have needed to for a long time. Give Thanos the place he deserves in the records of the Empire."

"Of course, your majesty," Cosmas intoned, reaching for his stylus once again.

"Thank you," Claudius said, although he'd always thought that kings didn't thank people for doing what they were commanded. Perhaps it was time to change that too. "If you need me, I will be back in my chambers, dealing with the other half of this."

"The other half of this, your majesty?"

Claudius nodded.

"I need to summon my other son and tell him."

"Tell him what, your majesty?"

There came a long silence, and finally Claudius replied.

"That he is no longer my heir."

CHAPTER EIGHTEEN

Stephania sat alone in her chambers, looking out over the city, holding the small vial up to the light, as a tear ran down her cheek. She pondered the clear liquid, wondering, debating.

It was the same spot where she'd been sitting when Lucious had come to her to offer it to her. Take this, he'd said, and she would no longer be carrying Thanos's child. Take this, he'd said, and she would be free to form the marriage alliance with him he wanted.

The thought of that made Stephania feel sick, and not just in the ways that had been plaguing her since the start of this pregnancy. She knew what Lucious was better than anyone. The thought of marriage to him was abhorrent, vile. The fact that he'd tried to woo her rather than simply forcing himself on her the way he usually did with women barely made it better. Any relationship with him would not be a thing of equals, whatever he said.

Yet Stephania still found herself considering the vial.

Part of it was that she could see which way the wind was blowing. Lucious had all but won the war against the rebellion. He would be the next king and Stephania suspected that his good will toward her would only last so long. Perhaps her only option was to side with him, however much she despised him.

Then there was the other object of her hatred, her love... Stephania still wasn't sure where one stopped and the other began. Thanos had abandoned her. How much would it hurt him to know that she had aborted their child? To know that she had done it because he had walked away?

Stephania opened the vial, sniffing at it. She had already tested it to make sure that it was what Lucious claimed it to be. She wouldn't put it past him to poison her, and make it look as though she'd killed herself out of grief. Yet there was no reason for him to do that when he could simply have revealed her role in Thanos's escape, or let her go.

One long draught and it would be done. Stephania lifted the vial in a silent toast. Only a knock at the door interrupted her.

"What is it?" Stephania demanded, corking the vial and setting it down.

One of her hand maidens entered. This one was called... Elethe, wasn't she? A girl with soft tan skin, dark eyes, and delicately painted designs on each cheek that varied by the day. She'd been a traveler from Felldust who had made herself useful at court, and quickly found a place in Stephania's entourage. She made an adequate replacement for those lost in the attempts to free Thanos. Not that Lucious had executed any, but the ones who had given away her secrets couldn't be trusted again, could they?

"My lady," the girl said. "There have been reports coming in that we thought you would want to hear about."

Stephania dragged her attention away from thoughts of revenge. "What have you heard?"

"There are several things, my lady," Elethe said. She closed her eyes, and Stephania guessed that she was getting things in order. She liked her girls to keep information in their heads so that there would be no traces. "First, you should know that messages have come in suggesting that Prince Thanos is returning to Delos."

Stephania's breath caught at that, and she hated the way a part of her responded with happiness even after all he'd done. "You're certain?"

"Some of the messages came from Haylon, where he had traveled. There was also a bird from fishers in the waters beyond the city."

So, Thanos was coming back. Stephania tried to work out what that meant, both for her and for Delos. She could think of the obvious reason why he would have returned, of course.

"Ceres," she said. "He's come back for Ceres."

Just the thought of that made anger rise in her, fresh and hot. Only the thought that Lucious had probably had Ceres killed by now made her hold back. When Elethe cleared her throat, Stephania caught her with a glare so harsh that the woman took a step back.

"What?" she demanded.

"There's more, my lady. Obviously we do not have the contacts with the guards that we did…"

Because Stephania had already expended most of her favors among the guards getting Thanos out, and because the guards were more cautious now.

"But it seems," Elethe went on, "that Ceres has escaped. The rumor is that there are now four statues where guards attempted to kill her."

"Blood of the Ancient Ones," Stephania said, making a curse out of it even though it was really nothing more than an observation. She should have known that Ceres wouldn't be so easily contained. The simple fact of her capture had seemed like proof that these things could be stopped.

She should have known better. Ceres had escaped once. Of course she would escape again. She should have made sure.

Looking at Elethe, though, she could see that wasn't everything the girl had to say.

"There's more?" she said.

Her handmaiden nodded. "The king... the king has made an announcement. In public, he has said that he intends to undo many of the harsh measures put in place to counter the rebellion. He did not mention Prince Lucious's new Killings in the Stade, but he spoke on many other matters."

"And in private?" Stephania asked.

"One of the others was listening near the Hall of Scholars. She heard the king order Cosmas to put Thanos back in the records... as his firstborn son. He intends to make him his heir, and he has sent for Lucious."

Somehow, that fact was the one that pushed Stephania over the edge of her anger. She picked up the vial Lucious had given her, intending to gulp it down, then stopped. She stepped over to her room's balcony, then flung it from herself, so that it glittered for a moment in the sunlight before arching down to the cobbles below. If servants looked up in surprise, they at least had the sense not to say anything.

"My lady?" Elethe said. "Are you well?"

"Well?" Stephania rounded on her. She backhanded her handmaiden, feeling the crack of her knuckles across the girl's cheek. "You've just told me that at the point when it seemed as though things might finally be settled, everything has changed, and you ask me if I'm *well*?"

"I... forgive me, my lady." Elethe was on her knees. Good. It was nice to know that at least someone there was going to remember that Stephania still had some power.

Stephania touched the spot she'd struck, as gently as she could. "No, forgive me. I know that you are loyal to me, aren't you?"

"Completely. I will do whatever you require, my lady."

One day, Stephania would probably test that. For now, though, she had simpler requests. She'd spent too much time acting based on her emotions, as if she were some kind of animal, or worse, like Lucious. How would he be taking the news that he wasn't heir? Did he even know yet? Following her emotions had been the mistake she'd made with trying to help Thanos. If she'd just been ruthless about it when she had the chance, none of this would have happened.

Well, now was the time to make up for that.

"Bring me writing materials," Stephania said.

The girl did, and Stephania set to work, laying them out in front of her, dipping a quill in ink and trying to think of the words that would have the greatest effect. They were such subtle weapons, used well. They couldn't cut through flesh or stop hearts, but they could persuade people to do both those things, and they could certainly break a heart.

It was just a matter of working out what to write. Stephania smiled to herself at the thought that the most effective approach to this would probably be the simplest. Most of the time, she did her work through secrecy and lies, but people sometimes underestimated just how big a weapon the truth could be, if set out the right way.

So Stephania set it out, step by step. The fact that Thanos was returning. The conjecture that the king intended to give him the throne. From there, it was only a small step to make it sound less like a reconciliation and more like an attempt to destroy the natural order of things. She didn't include any suggestions as to what to do about it, of course. That would have been a step too far, and Stephania had learned the hard way that her intended recipient didn't take well to being told what to do.

Besides, she didn't need to. She could guess at Lucious's reactions, as easily as she could guess what would happen if she threw a hawk into a dovecote. She'd had enough of being stuck here, reacting to events, caught first by Thanos's failure to tell her everything and then by Lucious's machinations.

It was time to start taking control of things again.

"Take this letter and have one of the others deliver it to Lucious," Stephania said. "Do not do it yourself, because he will be angry once he reads it, and I will have better things for you to do than being hurt by him. Send one of the girls who spoke too much before. Let them think they're regaining my trust."

He would probably torture whoever she sent, just to prove that he could. Or maybe he would think that the girl was a conduit to her thoughts. Yes, that had possibilities, and Stephania was enjoying the fact that she was seeing those possibilities again. She was coming back to herself, the weakness that had come from her love for Thanos forgotten.

If she set Thanos and Lucious against one another, with the king in the middle, she was the only one guaranteed to come out as a winner. She was carrying the heir to the throne's child, but she was also the one to warn Lucious. But she wanted to make sure.

"We still have enough watchers to tell us when Thanos approaches the docks?" Stephania asked.

"Yes, my lady."

"Then you will be going to him. Come here, let me see you."

Elethe stood before her, and Stephania considered the look that she required. The blow she'd delivered before was blooming nicely into a bruise. She reached out thoughtfully and tore the girl's dress with a jerk. Yes, that was better. She could have done more, but it was best to be subtle about these things.

"Perfect," Stephania said. "The bruise will make this work nicely."

Better to let the girl think that it was all part of a plan than that Stephania had simply lashed out. It would do more to secure her loyalty.

"There are things I require you to say to Thanos," Stephania said. "Things I want you to be sure you remember." She leaned forward and whispered, even though she could have spoken. It reinforced how much she was taking the girl into her confidence. Stephania smiled at how easily all this was coming back to her. She would not sit there and be helpless. She would *not* be defeated like this.

"Do you understand?" Stephania asked when she was done.

"I will remember every word," Elethe said.

"You must do more than that. You must convince him. You can do that, can't you? I would hate to think I'd put my trust in the wrong person."

"I will make you proud, my lady."

"I'm sure you will," Stephania said.

Now, there was just the question of Ceres. There was a part of her that wanted to be simple and practical about it. To assume that the Empire would deal with her in time. Yet it was hard to believe that, when she had already escaped twice. And this was practical. After all Stephania had taunted her with, there was no doubt that Ceres would seek revenge. It was what Stephania would have done, after all.

"While you are gone," Stephania said, "I will require another of the girls to attend me while I make a journey into the city."

"Is that entirely safe, my lady?" Elethe asked.

If Stephania hadn't heard the concern there, she might have struck the girl again, just to remind her not to question Stephania's instructions. As it was, she went to fetch her cloak, letting Elethe settle it around her shoulders while she tucked a spare knife into a sheath at the small of her back.

"If what you've said is true, then the streets will be safe for at least the next day or two as people try to work out what the king's pronouncement means for them. No one will quite trust it yet, and they won't want to risk anything."

It seemed so obvious to Stephania, when she put it like that, but her handmaiden still looked at her with surprise, as though only just learning the truth of her reasoning. It always came as a surprise to Stephania that others didn't realize these things the way she did.

"Don't worry," Stephania said, "I will take a girl who is good with knives."

"As you say, my lady," Elethe said. "Even so, if something happens, where should I look for you?"

Where should *she* look? Stephania smiled at that hint of protectiveness. She'd always been so good at inspiring loyalty. Or she'd thought she was. She hadn't been able to inspire it in Thanos, thanks to Ceres.

She would be dealing with her soon enough, though.

"There is a certain witch in the Tangled quarter," Stephania said. "They say that she knows many things, and I plan to find out exactly how much."

"What could some witch have to teach *you*, my lady?" Elethe asked.

"Oh, all kinds of things," Stephania said with a smile.

Things such as how to kill an Ancient One safely, without the risk of being turned to stone.

CHAPTER NINETEEN

Ceres, still soaking wet from her jump, barely felt the water dripping from her as she walked the city in a daze. People looked her way as she passed, but so long as none of them were guards, she didn't care. She didn't even care about the pulse of energy within her, there again after going missing for so long.

She was too busy looking at the damage in the city, the carnage that remained after their assault on the gate.

She should have been happy to be free, but how could she be happy when there were so many others who had lost everything? Their freedom, their lives, all given up in her cause.

Ceres walked down toward the gate where they'd entered. She kept from the main streets while she did it, but other than that, she didn't try to hide. Right then, she would almost have welcomed the chance to fight with the guards who must surely be hunting her by now.

That leached away though as she started to see the damage in the city.

It started with broken windows and cracked plasterwork. An arrow lodged in the chimney stack of a house, obviously sticking there as one of her riders tried to return fire. It looked strangely lonely to Ceres, less evidence of a battle than the tale of one man, who had probably found himself cut down moments later. It was easier to mourn for one man somehow than for the thought of a host of them.

Ceres saw more evidence of the violence as she got closer. There was a bloodstain on one of the walls nearby, drying now into darkness against the wattle and daub. A stab of sadness shot through Ceres then, mixed in with guilt and anger at the thought that she'd brought them to this. She'd led them into the city, so sure it was her destiny. She'd been a part of their deaths as surely as Lucious had.

She saw Empire uniforms ahead and realized that she *didn't* want to fight then. There had been enough deaths. Instead, Ceres hurried across to a set of stairs leading up to a flat roof, keeping low now as she progressed. She had to see this, and she had to see all of it.

Below, she could see soldiers, probably conscripts, dragging away bodies. Even after the time Ceres had spent locked away, there were too many to count. There were a few imperial uniforms mixed in, and a few more bodies Ceres recognized as members of the rebellion, but overwhelmingly, they wore the colors of Lord West's forces.

Even as Ceres watched, a group of them descended on the next body, stripping away anything of value before throwing it on a cart. They did it so casually that Ceres could only stand there, trying to hold in her anger at the lack of respect.

She kept moving, hopping to the next rooftop. A glimpse of imperial armor up there suggested that at least one of the archers firing down at Lord West's men had been hit, but that was no kind of comfort.

Below, she could see more soldiers taking apart the barricades they had built, ordinary people joining them to take back doors and tables, barrels and benches as they picked apart the joins that had held them. More seemed to be patching their homes, repairing the damage done as desperate soldiers fought to get away. Ceres saw one man contemplating a largely burnt out house, obviously trying to make some sense of it.

There was so much destruction there, but those who had died out here in the streets had probably still been better off than the ones Lucious had gotten his hands on. Ceres had to lean against the edge of the roof as she remembered the look on Anka's face while the life had slipped from her. She thought of Lord West, who had only been there at all because he had believed in the power her blood gave her.

Power that hadn't come when Ceres needed it.

"What use am I if I can't save anyone?" Ceres asked.

She needed to know then if anyone had survived. Looking down, it seemed almost impossible that they had. She had to check, though, and that meant finding her way down to the rebellion's tunnels and hideaways.

She kept to the shadows while she moved, looking for the entrances she remembered. Too many had soldiers near them, not guarding them, but working there. Some were filling in holes, bricking up entrances. Ceres saw others carrying out boxes and bags of possessions, obviously whatever had been left behind by the rebellion.

She had to creep around for at least half an hour more before she found an entrance that appeared unguarded. It was little more than a crack with a rough slope behind it, leading down into what lay beneath. Ceres scrambled down carefully, finding herself in the tunnels that the rebellion had made its own.

It was quiet there in a way that it hadn't been before. The last time she'd been there, there had been so many people that there was always some sound in the background, no matter what else was happening.

She made her way through the near darkness of the tunnels, looking for any signs of habitation. It seemed more like a ghost town than a lived in place, though. Anka had taken so many of her people with her to fight, and now… what was left? Possessions left in the dirt for owners who would never return? Food left half finished, in some cases, already starting to go bad.

Ceres heard voices in the dark and advanced toward them. She saw candlelight, and approached that glow cautiously, seeing an older woman with a couple of children there in a room that looked as though it had already been picked clean.

Ceres saw her look up as she approached, and the older woman pushed the children behind her, drawing a knife.

"You don't have to worry about me," Ceres said, holding up her hands. "I'm not here to hurt you."

"If you're who I think you are," the woman said, "you're the reason this place is empty."

"That wasn't me," Ceres replied, although she knew it *was* her fault. "We were betrayed."

"I heard that," the woman admitted. "Me and the children came down here because there wasn't anywhere else to go after all the fighting. When they didn't come back, I had to try to find a way to survive, and I figured it was empty anyway. Soldiers came round. We stayed ahead of them."

"Are there others here?" Ceres asked.

The other woman shrugged. "A few. They've been telling me things. Apparently, the king has announced that it's all over."

Ceres didn't know what to feel about that. On the one hand, peace was good, but it couldn't be at any price. The king couldn't just decide that the rebellion was done with.

"Does he think they've finally killed enough?" she asked.

That got another shrug. "Maybe. People have started filtering back into the tunnels. The king ordered them let go."

A brief flash of hope flared then. This wasn't done.

"Lord West's men?" Ceres asked. "The combatlords?"

"They say the nobles they released headed out of the city," the woman said. "That they want to meet up with any of their friends still left outside and go home. The combatlords…"

There was something about the way she said it that made fear rise in Ceres's chest.

"What happened?" she said.

"Lucious announced they were going to have one great games at the Stade," the woman said. "The king stopped the rest of it, but that... I think it's still happening. People say they're just slaves anyway, and it's what they're there for."

"So why not kill them all as one great sacrifice for peace?" Ceres guessed. No one would want to try to stop it, because of the risks of restarting the conflict. They would stand by. They would probably even watch.

Unless she did something.

"You said that Lord West's men are outside the city?" Ceres said. "Do you know your way through the tunnels to the outside?"

***

When Ceres had first arrived at the city with Lord West, their army's camp had been a wonder to behold, stretching almost to the horizon, filled with shining armor and fluttering banners.

Now, it looked like bones that were in the process of being picked clean, and the contrast was heartbreaking. Ceres saw men there: riders and their attendants, battered-looking warriors in dented armor. Many were injured, and even the ones who weren't had a haunted look to them as they packed away what they could of their camp, getting ready to go.

Ceres could feel the hostility there from the moment she walked into the camp. It was there with every step, in the stares that followed her, quickly replacing any looks of surprise.

A group of the soldiers stepped forward, headed by a man with a reddish beard, whose armor still looked pristine. Ceres didn't recognize him from the battle, though there had been so many men there at the start that it would have been impossible to remember them all.

"What are you doing here?" he demanded. His hand rested on the hilt of his sword.

"What are *you* doing?" Ceres countered. "Better yet, *who* are you?"

"I am Nyel de Langolin, third cousin to Lord West, protector of the lands around the village of Upper Flewt, and second rider at the trials of the north eastern grasses. I know who you are. You're the one who led my cousin to ruin."

That stung at Ceres, but she kept her temper, not least because this man had every reason to blame her. She blamed herself, but there was no time to think like that.

"You're packing up?" Ceres demanded, looking around at the camp. Everywhere she looked, men seemed to be salvaging what they could from tents and getting the remains of their weaponry in order. Most were packing it away in a way that made it clear they weren't preparing for another fight.

"What else should they be doing?" Nyel said. "You led them in a suicidal charge against the city, and they lost. The king has declared the fighting over, and it is only because of his graciousness that most of them have their lives. If I had been there when you came to Lord West's keep, I would have advised him against this foolishness."

"And where were you?" Ceres asked. "Where were you when the rest of us were marching here? Where were you while we were risking our lives? Your armor looks remarkably *clean* to have been anywhere near the fighting."

She saw him go almost as red as his beard at that.

"How dare you, girl! We received my cousin's message late, and then we were caught up on the road. Had we known the dire straits you would bring our forces to, we would have found a way to save you from yourselves!"

In other words, he'd hung back, wanting an excuse not to be part of it all. Ceres ignored him then, turning to the others and raising her voice so that the men packing away their tents would hear.

"Listen to me, all of you! This is not the time to leave. We aren't finished here."

"Finished," Nyel said. "Of course you're finished. The king has declared the conflict over."

"King Claudius doesn't get to decide when we stop fighting," Ceres replied. "Especially not when his son is about to slaughter the combatlords. The king might not know about that, but they'll be just as dead when Lucious is done."

"Slaves and brutes," Nyel said. "You expect these men to risk their lives for them?"

"I expect you all to honor the oath you gave to me, and to Lord West!" Ceres replied. By now, a crowd of men was starting to gather around her. She talked to them, not to Lord West's conveniently delayed cousin.

"We still have a chance to win this," Ceres said. "We were beaten at the gate by treachery, but the barricades they used are coming down. The army isn't prepared now. The evils of the Empire don't disappear simply because the king has declared victory. With the combatlords and what's left of the rebellion, we could still do this. At the very least, we could get the combatlords to safety."

"So what do you want us to do?" Nyel countered. "Charge in there on glittering steeds to assault the city? Look at the men around you. *Look* at them. They have tried that once. They put their trust in you once. Look what it cost them."

Ceres knew exactly what it had cost everyone who had followed her. She knew what the rebellion had cost *her*. She still had no idea if her brother or father were safe, while thoughts of Rexus, Anka, Garrant, and everyone else who'd died haunted her dreams.

"You swore oaths," Ceres said, but she knew that wouldn't work. She couldn't force these men to fight for her.

"Lord West put his stock in oaths," one of the men around her said. "Look what happened."

"And we swore to you as one of the Ancient Ones," another shouted. "But when the time came, your powers did nothing."

Ceres could see the pain there on the faces of the men who'd fought. She tried appealing to them one last time.

"Please," she called out to the soldiers around her. "Good men are going to die down there in the Stade, when they could be helping us to bring an end to the Empire. I know what happened last time. I was there, in the middle of it, but that's no reason to stop. This is a moment to act!"

She expected at least some response to that. If not a rousing cheer, then at least a few men willing to step forward or announce that they were with her. Instead, Ceres found herself greeted with silence.

"It seems you have your answer," Nyel said.

It seemed she did, but Ceres couldn't let the men in the Stade die.

The combatlords were going to die, and she couldn't let that happen.

She turned and set off, heading back toward the city, alone, and prepared to face her death.

CHAPTER TWENTY

Thanos's heart was in his mouth as Felene guided them into Delos's harbor. He could see the tension in her too as she held the tiller, their boat slipping between the merchant vessels and the galleys, the fishing boats and the smaller skiffs.

"It's been a long time since I came into Delos this openly," Felene said. "I keep expecting to find a row of guards waiting for us on the docks."

Thanos knew exactly how she felt. He was returning to a city he'd only escaped from with difficulty, and where, for all he knew, the guards might have been ordered to kill him on sight. He knew he had to show confidence though. This had been his idea, after all.

"Just keep your head down," Thanos said. "It will be fine."

"You need to work on your lying," Felene told him. "You're terrible at it."

"I kept secret the fact that I was helping the rebellion," Thanos said. "I lied to generals and courtiers. I lied to my own family."

"All for this Ceres girl," Felene said. "She must be something special."

Thanos bit back a flash of annoyance, because it was true. Ceres was special. But he'd become involved with the rebellion for more than just her.

"I did it because it was the right thing to do," Thanos said. The same way that coming back for Stephania was right, whatever she'd done. Whatever else had happened since.

"It's a rare thing these days to find a noble who thinks like that," Felene said. "I'm glad I'm a thief and a killer. It makes things a lot simpler."

Thanos doubted it was that simple for her. After all, she'd been the one to talk him into this.

He saw her nod toward the docks. "Looks as though there's at least one person waiting. I've changed course twice, and they've moved so they're on the part of the dock I'm heading for."

Thanos looked, and saw a figure in a cloak there near the edge of the dock. He had the impression of a female figure, and for a moment, hope rose up in him. Maybe it was Stephania, there waiting to escape. Maybe they would be able to do this and get away before anyone noticed. Maybe he wouldn't have to offer up his own life.

As they got closer, though, he could see it wasn't Stephania. He knew her figure by now, the way she stood, the way she did things.

Stephania would never have waited looking that frightened for anyone. Even with her life in danger, she would have stood as if she owned the world around her. This was someone else.

"Should I get ready to fight?" Felene asked. Thanos could see her looking around the buildings that ringed the docks, obviously searching for potential attackers.

Thanos waved her back. There wasn't anyone else there. No, this was something else.

"I'll tie up the boat," Thanos said, taking the line as they approached. "Be ready if anything happens."

He felt the moment when the boat bumped against the wood of the dock, leaping out lightly and tying the boat into place. There was a risk in that moment, because if the cloaked figure turned out to be an assassin, Thanos was offering her his back. He had to trust that Felene would intervene if that did happen.

Yet it didn't. The cloaked figure was still standing there when Thanos turned back to her. She took a step forward, pulling back the hood of her cloak. She was a young woman Thanos didn't know, with softly tan skin, dark hair cut short, and dark eyes. Thanos could see a bruise blooming into a rainbow of colors on one of her cheeks, while her expensive-looking dress was torn as if she'd ripped free from someone's grip.

"Prince Thanos," she said, and Thanos could hear her breath catch with what sounded like relief. "Thank the gods. I wasn't sure if it would really be you coming, or if this would just be one of Prince Lucious's traps."

"Lucious?" Thanos said with a frown. "What's going on? What are you doing here? Who are you?"

"And are we about to have a hundred guards coming down on us?" Felene asked from behind him in a much harder tone. Thanos saw the girl flinch at it.

"My name... my name is Elethe. I'm one of Lady Stephania's handmaidens."

Thanos saw Felene hop up from the boat, quickly jumping behind the girl and wrapping an arm around her throat. Her hand delved into the cloak, coming out with a dagger.

"Sent to kill Thanos and anyone with him? Give me one reason I shouldn't put this blade through your ribs."

"I'm not here for that!" Elethe insisted, squirming in Felene's grip.

Thanos raised a hand. "That's enough, Felene. Assassins don't usually come looking as though they've just escaped from something."

96

"You didn't spend enough time on the Isle of Prisoners if you believe that," Felene countered, but she let Elethe go.

"You still didn't say what you were doing here," Thanos said. Felene might think that he was being too trusting, but he wasn't blind when it came to Stephania, or the plots that dominated Delos.

"I… I managed to get away," the girl said. "When they came for Lady Stephania, they tried to take me too. I've been hiding since then, listening to whatever rumors I could, trying to find a way to help. Some of Lady Stephania's old informants… they told me you were coming. They heard it from people… on Haylon."

Thanos saw tears spring to her eyes then. She certainly sounded as though she were scared for her life, although given the threat Felene had made, it was hard to tell for sure.

"All right," Thanos said. "Calm down. Relax. You're safe now. No one is going to hurt you."

They took her to the boat, sitting her down in it so that they could talk without being caught out on the street if it turned out that guards had followed her. Thanos could see her looking around anxiously, as if expecting things to go wrong at any minute.

"You need to tell us everything," Thanos insisted. "What happened with Stephania? Why were guards coming for her? The last I saw of her, Lucious said he wouldn't let that happen."

"And you believed him?" Felene asked.

She was right, of course. Thanos cursed himself for a fool, for trusting Lucious even that much. For telling himself that he didn't care what happened to Stephania, when the very fact that he was here told him that he did. Part of that was honor, but it had to be more than that, didn't it?

"Prince Lucious came to Lady Stephania with a vial that would destroy the child inside her," Elethe went on. "He told her that she would continue to be safe only if she took it, and if she put you aside."

"Stephania wouldn't do that," Thanos said, but even as he said it, he realized that he had no idea what Stephania would and wouldn't do. He hadn't thought that she would send an assassin after him, after all.

"She was angry after you left," Elethe said, and that had the ring of truth to it. "She was grieving for you the way I've never seen her before. I think… I think you were the only thing she really cared about, and you were gone."

A wave of guilt hit Thanos at that, because he knew it was true. Whatever else she was, Stephania had loved him, and he had

97

abandoned her. He had sailed away, leaving her with Lucious. He had done this, as much as her.

"Are you saying..." he began, but he couldn't even bring himself to ask it.

Elethe seemed to understand what he wanted to know, though, because Thanos saw her nod. That brought a fresh burst of pain, even before she said the next words.

"Lady Stephania... she took the potion. She formally set you aside. She didn't have a choice."

Thanos reeled in a way that made it feel as though the boat he was on were suddenly enveloped in a storm. He felt Felene's hand on his arm, and shook her off. This wasn't the kind of thing anyone could help him with. It felt right then as though the whole world had disappeared from beneath him.

In a way, it had. Just a short while ago, he had been a married man, with everything ahead of him and a child on the way. Now both of those things had been torn away from him so abruptly that it seemed impossible. It was too much. It was too soon.

That was one of the biggest parts of it. Thanos had hardly had time to become used to the idea of being married before it had all been gone. The idea of being a father had been like a dream coming to him and then snatched away almost as quickly. He'd never even had time to think about what it might be like.

He thought now, and even dreaming about it hurt with the promise of what could have been. He could have had a son, and raised him to be the kind of noble the world needed, showing him how to use a sword but also teaching him what was right, and kind, and good. Thanos could imagine himself with the boy, teaching him to ride, and fight, but also to think, and stand up for those weaker than himself. He could have had a daughter, and... well, why not teach her all the things he would have taught a son? Ceres had shown him that a woman could use a blade every bit as well as a man.

He could imagine what their daughter would have been like. As beautiful and as intelligent as Stephania, but hopefully with Thanos's commitment to others, and his need to make the Empire a better place for those who lived in it. Picturing it made his heart ache, because he knew it could never happen now, because of what Lucious had pushed Stephania into doing.

Because of what *he* had pushed her into doing. If he hadn't left her behind, none of this would have happened. Stephania had told him that things could be different, that *she* could be different, and in his anger Thanos had robbed them both of the chance of a future.

When he looked up at the two women in the boat with him, it was as though he was coming back to himself from a long way away. He could barely remember what he was doing there, let alone what he needed to ask next.

Thankfully, Felene asked it for him. "If Stephania did what Lucious wanted, then why would guards come after her? What kind of lie are you spinning?"

"No lie," Elethe insisted. "Lady Stephania did what Lucious required, but there were other things she *wouldn't* do. She wouldn't go to his bed. She wouldn't be his mistress or get involved in the… things he was doing. In revenge, Lucious told the king about her role in helping you to escape."

"And King Claudius had her taken?" Thanos asked.

He saw Elethe nod. "Her and any of her handmaidens who were there. Lucious claimed those. I managed to get away, but… I heard the king is imprisoning Stephania in one of the most secure towers of the castle until he decides what to do about her. He's angry, Prince Thanos. He's *very* angry."

Thanos felt something he hadn't believed he would feel then: pity for Stephania, and fear on her behalf. There was a part of him that said Stephania deserved whatever fate she got after all the people she'd killed, all the times she'd manipulated people. Yet there was more of him that knew he had to find a way to make this right. He had to find a way to save her, before the worst happened.

And it would happen. Thanos was the king's own son, and King Claudius had been going to have him either executed or sent to the Isle of Prisoners. Stephania would suffer at least the same, if not worse.

"You're sure she isn't dead already?" Thanos asked. That would be the cruelest thing of all: to know that he'd come this far, without any hope of saving her in the end.

Elethe shook her head. "I don't know anything for sure, but I hear that the king is holding her. I think he is waiting for the nobles to agree with him about what should happen, or perhaps he is distracted with everything that has happened in the last few weeks. I don't know."

Thanos did. His father was holding her as a kind of hostage, knowing that eventually, Thanos would hear what had happened. He knew that Thanos would be coming for her, yet there was still only one thing to do.

"Felene, stay here with the boat. Make sure that there's a way out of here for Stephania when she comes."

"You mean for you and Stephania," Felene said.

"I hope so," Thanos replied, even though he knew it wouldn't work like that. "If you have to leave the harbor, try to sneak back in when you can."

"There's an old smuggler's landing outside the walls," Felene said. "If I can't get back here, I'll be there until I'm sure you're dead. I pay my debts."

Thanos nodded his thanks. "Elethe, stay with the boat. You'll be safe here."

"But—"

"Where else is there for you in the city?" Thanos asked. "Felene will keep you safe, and then we'll leave together."

"Oh, I'll look after her, right enough," Felene said. "And in the meantime, what exactly will you be doing, Thanos?"

The only thing he could do.

"I am going to see my father."

CHAPTER TWENTY ONE

Sartes let out a whoop of joy as the ox cart bounced its way down the road. He and Bryant were still going far faster than the oxen were probably used to, but for now, he reveled in it.

"We're free!" Bryant yelled beside him. "Free!"

Sartes smiled at that. The other boy seemed stronger just for having gotten away. Even if all the painful thinness and the marks of abuse were all still there, he had a sense of hope to him now that made it seem less likely that he might collapse at any moment. Sartes suspected he looked much the same. He certainly felt like he never wanted this moment to end.

Even so, he knew it had to. Eventually, they would have to slow the cart down, if only to stop the oxen from tiring before they got where they were going.

They would need to work that out too. Sartes didn't know whether they could return to Delos or not and if not there, where could they go? Sartes didn't like the idea of going anywhere but Delos though. That was where Ceres was, and his father. He still didn't know what had happened with the attack. Maybe they'd pulled back. Maybe they'd even succeeded, but hadn't been able to find him, although Sartes doubted that. If they'd won, one of the first things the rebellion might have done would be to stop the cruelty of the tar pits.

Perhaps the battle for Delos was still continuing. It didn't matter. What mattered was that Sartes needed to see his family again and make sure that they were safe.

Before that, though, they needed food and water, and enough news to find out what was going on. Sartes didn't know where there was a safe place to find any of them. For the moment, they just had to keep going and hope. Even so, he slowed the oxen to a walk they could maintain, looking out across the horizon for any hint that might point them in the right direction.

Because of that, he spotted the slave line when it was still just a speck. It was unmistakable; men and women chained together and forced to walk by a quartet of guards, all overseen by a fat slaver riding on a cart. Just the sight of it made Sartes feel sick and frightened, all too aware of how vulnerable two boys on a cart might be.

It made him angry too, and that anger burned until it consumed all the rest of it.

"We need to get off the road," Sartes said. "Somewhere they can't see us."

He looked over the weapons they'd taken from the guard. They weren't much, surely not enough to take on four, maybe five, men? Yet he couldn't stand there and simply watch these people being dragged off into slavery, not when his mother had sold Ceres like that.

They pulled the cart off the road, finding a clump of trees to hide it behind. Sartes passed the reins to Bryant, letting the other boy hold the oxen still while Sartes took the guard's sword and watched the advancing group.

"They won't see us here, will they?" Bryant asked. "This is a good place to hide."

It was a good place to hide. Or a good place for an ambush. Sartes watched them getting closer, wanting to judge this right.

When he saw his father at the center of the line, his heart leapt into his mouth.

"Bryant, listen, we don't have much time," Sartes said. "My father's in that slave line. I can't leave him there."

"What do you need me to do?" Bryant asked, and Sartes could only feel grateful that he put it like that. It wasn't a question of what Sartes was going to do, but what they both were.

"I'm going to creep closer," Sartes said. "When I give you the signal, I need you to get those oxen moving. I need you to panic them if you can. After that... do whatever you can to get people away from the guards."

He saw Bryant swallow, and he didn't blame the other boy. Sartes was frightened too, but he couldn't just stand by.

He crept forward, to the leading edge of the stand of trees. He made sure to keep low, and the filth of the tar helped him here, blending him into the foliage so that Sartes was sure no one would spot him unless they stepped on him.

He waited while the group drew level with him. There were two guards at the front, dressed in what had probably once been imperial armor, but was now battered and patched. They flanked the wagon on which the slaver sat. Two more were at the back, driving the slave coffle on with whips.

Sartes could hear them talking to one another as they did it, and he crouched for a moment, listening, waiting.

"Looks as though we got out of the city just in time," one said. "The rebellion might be destroyed, but those new orders of the king's? Could be the last slave line for a while."

"There will always be slave lines," the other said. "Look at how many of these rebels Prince Lucious gave away. You think when he's king, there won't be all the work we could ever need?"

"Might be a while before then though," the first said. "And he killed plenty of them. It's a waste."

"Just means there's no glut in the market," the second replied.

"But just think of all the combatlords he's having killed in the Stade! If he'd given us them, we'd make a fortune!"

"And the boss would have to hire a dozen more men, so how much of it would you and I see?"

Sartes had heard enough. The line was almost in position. It was time to act.

"Now!" he yelled, and then ran forward. Surprise was his only hope then. He just had to trust that Bryant would do all that Sartes had asked.

The first of the guards was turning toward him by then, but Sartes was already stabbing with his stolen sword. Between his father and the army, he'd learned more than enough about where the gaps in imperial armor were. His sword slid in under the guard's arm, and the man stumbled back, looking almost shocked at what had happened as he fell.

Sartes heard a crash and the cries of animals, and glanced back to see their wagon careening into that of the slaver. One of the guards lay in the dirt, obviously having been struck by it, while Sartes saw the slaver leap from the cart and stumble.

Perhaps because he was expecting it, he recovered quicker than the second guard, turning back to him and slicing his sword across the man's leg.

"You'll die for that, pup!" the guard bellowed and lunged forward, but the cut to his leg slowed him. Sartes was able to dance aside, striking again while his opponent stumbled. This time, Sartes caught him in the throat.

He ran for the front of the column, seeing Bryant being pushed back by a guard while the slaver lay on his back, shouting instructions and pointing.

"Don't just stand there! Kill him! What do I pay you for?"

Sartes ran past him, ignoring the man while he buried his sword in the last guard's back. He heard the man gasp, then fall forward, just short of the spot where Bryant stood with only a knife.

The other boy looked awed. "Four men," Bryant said. "You managed to kill four men!"

Sartes shook his head. "One was hit by the cart, and I took the rest by surprise."

Even so, the boy continued to look at him as though he was a combatlord. Was this what Ceres felt like, with people looking at her as if she could do anything?

Right then, he had more important things to deal with. The slaver was still on his back, and his earlier confidence had given way to fear.

"Don't kill me!" the man said. "Please don't kill me!"

"Where are the keys to the chains?" Sartes demanded, leveling his sword. The sight of blood on the blade made him feel sick, but he forced himself to stay as terrifying as he could be. "Give me them. Now!"

"Here... here!" The slaver threw him a bunch of keys. "You're not going to kill me, are you?"

"I'm not going to kill you," Sartes said. He gestured to the chained figures behind the cart. "I'm going to unchain everyone. I can't make any promises about what *they'll* do though."

He watched the slaver start to run, hobbling away from the road on one good leg. Somehow, there was far more satisfaction in that than there would have been in stabbing the man.

He hurried to his father first, and there were no words to say. He could only wrap his arms around him.

"I thought you were dead!" his father said. "When you didn't come back, I was sure that you had to be."

"I tried to get back to you all," Sartes said, and joy welled up in him at the fact that his father was there safe and alive. Swiftly, he unlocked the chains, letting them fall away and then tossing the keys to the next prisoner.

They freed one another, whooping in joy at their freedom.

"You saved them," his father said. "You saved all of us. I'm proud of you, son."

The others gathered there around them. Some of them reached out to touch Sartes with a hand on his shoulder, a palm pressed into his. It seemed as though everyone there needed something other than words for how grateful they were. Sartes could understand that. If someone had freed him from the prison cart, he wouldn't have had the words either.

"I wish we'd never been parted," he told his father.

"It's probably just as well you weren't there," his father said. "We were betrayed, Sartes."

Sartes stared blankly at his father. "Who... what happened?"

"They grabbed us while we tried to open the gate. After that... Sartes, I'm so sorry, but Anka's dead."

Pain flashed through Sartes then. Anka had been the person who had seen the potential in him within the rebellion. She'd been the one to make things better for all of them. Now she was gone, and Sartes could barely believe it.

"What about Ceres?" Sartes asked. He wouldn't be able to bear it if she was gone too.

"I don't know," his father admitted. "I wish I had better news for you." He looked around. "We need to work out what we're going to do now. The rebellion is gone. We need to decide where might be safe."

Sartes had an answer for that. "I heard the guards talking. Lucious is planning to kill the combatlords at the Stade. We can still help them." He found himself thinking of Anka, and of Ceres. This was the kind of thing they would do. The kind of thing they *had* done.

"Sartes, you've done amazing work saving us," his father said, "but the Stade is different. There will be more guards there. We don't even have a way to get close."

Sartes looked at the slaver's cart, wondering if it would roll. He hefted the chains.

"I think we do."

CHAPTER TWENTY TWO

Ceres approached the Stade with her anger and her need to save the combatlords both burning brightly. She reeled at the enormity of the task before her. Could she even reach the Stade? There were always ways through the streets of the city without being seen. The hard part would be getting inside. It was too much to hope that she wouldn't be recognized, and as for getting in there with weapons....

Ceres shook her head.

No, there's no way to do it.

She had to *find* a way, though, which was why she kept moving in the direction of the Stade.

Already, she could see the crowds gathering in the streets, waiting for the beginning of the games. She'd heard so much about the king supposedly pulling back from the brutality that had gone before, yet either that was a lie, Lucious hadn't heard what was expected of him, or he'd simply ignored his father.

Ceres didn't care which. Whatever it was, it told her that the Empire's promises of peace couldn't be trusted.

She blended with the crowd as best she could while she made her way closer. She could sense the unease there. People still weren't certain if this was a trick or not. Probably they didn't like the idea that the king just got to declare their rebellion over. Yet they seemed to be moving toward the Stade in an orderly enough fashion. They still seemed to want the violence of the Killings.

Maybe there was a kind of twisted cleverness to Lucious in these games. The people of the city had been built up to expect violence. That wouldn't just go away without some kind of release. The Killings would do that while setting things back in their old order.

Ceres shuffled along with the crowd as long as she dared, but it was soon obvious that she wouldn't just be walking into the Stade. There were too many guards around, lining the route to it and in some cases mingling with the crowd. Ceres saw a squad of the men approaching and thought she might have been discovered, yet they veered off at the last minute to grab two men who had started a scuffle a little way over. It seemed they would allow no violence but their own there.

As if to confirm that, there were tables set up outside the Stade, with a smattering of weapons spread out on them, and guards looking on nearby. Officials took weapons from the few who had brought them, only letting them through into the Stade once they were disarmed. Ceres had no doubt that they would recognize her, even if others hadn't so far.

"There has to be another way in," Ceres muttered, continuing on her way around the Stade. She knew the back ways in, the ways they let in the combatlords and the provisions for the days of the Killings. Instinct told her that one of those had to offer a better opportunity than trying to go in through the front.

So she tried it, only to find that someone else was already trying it. A slaver's cart sat by the entrance, the occupants arguing with guards while a line of chained figures trailed behind, obviously as more fodder for the Stade.

The sight of that was enough to make Ceres abandon her caution. These slaves deserved her help as much as those in the Stade. She charged.

***

"I'm telling you," Sartes heard his father say. "We're here for the Killings."

From his place on the cart, Sartes looked around, trying to find a better way in. It had seemed like such an obvious ploy when he'd thought of it. Pretend to be slavers delivering fresh meat to the Stade, and the guards would let them pass.

He hadn't anticipated so *many* guards, though, or that they would spend so long asking questions. If they looked too closely, they might even find the weapons hidden in the cart.

He saw the guard looking over the rebels in their chains. "This lot don't look much like combatlords to me."

"They're the warm-up," Sartes said. "Let the combatlords kill a few of these, get the crowd riled up, that sort of thing."

"They'll be more than riled up enough," the guard said. "Aren't you a little young for a mercenary?"

Sartes's breath caught, but he forced himself to keep going. He shrugged. "The army tried to conscript me, then the rebels tried to recruit me. You can see how that went."

"You're trying to tell me that *you* captured this lot?" the guard said. Sartes saw his frown deepen.

Maybe it was a lie too far. Sartes's hand tightened on his sword hilt.

A figure rushed past him, sword already blurring. Guards fell left and right. Bryant had looked at Sartes as though he was some kind of sword master for besting three guards by surprise, but *this* was pure skill. The figure ducked and wove, cut and sliced, while guards fell around her like corn in the harvest. Sartes stared as the last of them collapsed and the newcomer, spun, her sword rising.

"Ceres, wait! It's me, Sartes!"

He could barely believe it was really his sister there. He saw her stop, her sword poised, staring back at him in obvious shock as recognition hit her.

"Sartes? What are... Father? You're *both* alive? What are you doing here? What is this?"

Ceres looked as though she couldn't comprehend what was happening to her right then.

"We could ask you the same question," Sartes said. He rushed forward to hug her. "But I'm glad you're alive."

"It's good to see you too, little brother," Ceres assured him, and Sartes felt her ruffle his hair. "I take it you haven't really turned into a slaver while I've been locked away?"

"Do you like our disguises?" Sartes asked, and there was a boyish part of him that wanted to show off the cleverness of it to his sister, in spite of the darkness of everything that had happened. "We thought we might be able to help the combatlords."

"You were going to do that?" Ceres asked.

"You don't think we can?" Sartes countered. "We worked it out. If they think we're bringing in slaves, they'll let us right through. And if they don't, we can at least catch them by surprise." He sighed. "I know, it's a stupid idea, but we weren't expecting the ones here to argue so much."

He saw Ceres smile. "I think it's perfect. Especially now we're past the first line of them."

Sartes saw her slip into place in the line, handing over her sword so that their father could hide it in the cart. They started their shuffling walk toward the Stade again. They shuffled faster than they had, though, because they needed to get there before the aftermath of this fight might be discovered.

There were other reasons too. As the made their way into the workings of the Stade, Sartes could hear the calls of the crowd, and the blare of horns announcing the killing to come. The greatest games the Stade had seen had begun, and Sartes didn't know if they could get into the heart of the place in time to stop it.

CHAPTER TWENTY THREE

In spite of herself Ceres could feel her excitement building as the fake slave line made its way through the outer gates of the Stade. She could remember the last time she'd walked into this space. She could remember the sound of the crowd calling her name.

Even through the stone of the walls, she could hear a crowd now, its cries building in intensity as it demanded the violence to follow. Ceres could hear the emotion there, and she knew that either it could be sated the way Lucious wanted, or it could be turned toward something else.

They made it almost to the floor of the Stade before any guards challenged them. They rumbled through the outer gates without comment, then on through the inner workings of the arena. Only when they got to the iron gates leading to the sands did the guards there step in the way, drawing swords at the sight of them. Even they looked confused, as if this might still all be a mistake.

"You aren't supposed to be here," one said.

Ceres shook her head. "This is *exactly* where I'm supposed to be."

She threw off the chains that formed her disguise, rushed past the others, and slammed into the first guard. The impact of it was enough to knock him back into the wall beside it. He slid down it into unconsciousness.

Ceres was already moving. She stepped past the second guard's thrust, catching his sword and wrenching it from his hands. She threw him into the group of rebels with her, and she wasn't surprised to see a chain quickly wrapped around his throat, strangling him until he collapsed.

Ceres saw her brother start forward, but she shook her head. "Wait here, Sartes. I need you and the others to hold this exit, or we won't have a way out."

"But you can't go in there alone," Sartes insisted.

Ceres took the swords from the two guards, hefting one in either hand. "Trust me, little brother. I love you, and our father."

She took a breath and stepped out into the tunnel that led to the sands of the Stade. The closer she got, the more she could hear the cheers and the catcalls of the crowd, the sound washing over her like the roar of the ocean. On the sands, she could see men she recognized, combatlords she'd trained beside and who had been there with the rebellion.

109

They stood with their favored weapons in a loose circle, each too far from the next to reach quickly. Even the partial armor they normally wore in the Stade was gone, leaving them vulnerable and exposed. This wasn't a combat for them to survive.

Over it all, Ceres heard Lucious's voice calling down from the royal box.

"People of Delos. My subjects. Peasants. Today you get to witness the deaths of slaves and traitors. They die for your entertainment, but as more than that. Remember as you see them cut down the power of the Empire. Remember the price of rising against your rightful rulers!"

From where she was, Ceres could see Lucious standing on the balcony as a single golden point surrounded by mercenary bodyguards. Anger filled her then, at everything he was, at everything he'd done to her, her family and to the people of the Empire.

"These so-called combatlords will be permitted to fight for your amusement," Lucious said. "They will fight to the death, and the last to remain standing will be allowed to live, even given his freedom!"

Ceres saw the combat lords stand in place, looking at one another as though none wanted to be the first to move.

"If you will not fight, I will have you put down like the slaves you are," Lucious snapped. "I will have soldiers come in and execute you on your knees. Isn't it better to have a chance of living? Isn't it better to die on your feet?"

Ceres had put up with enough. She stepped out onto the sands, feeling them swirl up around her as the wind caught them.

"What will you really do with the last man, Lucious?" she called out, and at the sound of her voice, the Stade seemed to go uncomfortably silent around her. "Will you murder him quietly, the way you tried to with me? Will you say you changed your mind, the way you'll change your mind about holding back from hurting the common people? What will your excuse be?"

Ceres saw Lucious's eyes on her, and she could see the hatred there.

"Ceres, there you are," he called over the quiet of the Stade. "Don't you know when you're beaten? As for excuses... I'm a prince. I don't *need* any."

Ceres heard the whispers and the murmurs travelling around the Stade then. Questions, expressions of surprise, the need to know if it was really her. Ultimately, just one word came, again and again, subtle as the wind through a forest.

"Ceres. Ceres."

Lucious looked round in obvious anger at the sound of her name. "Enough," he yelled. "I'll have anyone chanting for her killed! As for the rest of you... the man who kills Ceres gets to live without fighting the rest!"

Ceres waited for the combatlords to descend on her. At least one would take Lucious's offer, and once one did, the rest would follow. Yet none moved. One, a barrel-chested man with a golden beard hanging almost to his waist, took one hand from the haft of an axe to make a rude gesture.

"You'll *give* us our freedom, will you?" he demanded. "And what kind of freedom would that be? I'll take my freedom, lad! I'll take it from you and all those like you, or die trying!"

Ceres knew an opportunity when she heard one.

"All of you," she called to the crowd. "Do *you* want to live only as long as Lucious gives you leave to? Do you want peace only until the next time the Empire chooses to take all that you have? They've given you peace, but the price is that nothing changes! *You* can change it, all of you!"

"The only thing that will change here," Lucious said, "is your shift into the land of the dead! If these slaves won't do it, my men will. Kill them all!"

Ceres heard the sound of horns, and gates opened around the Stade. It reminded her of the moments when they'd released great beasts for her to fight, except this time, armored men poured in. Soldier after soldier filed into the Stade, moving to encircle Ceres's group, cutting off their escape. Still they came.

"So many," one of the combatlords said.

Ceres heard another laugh. "Well, I wouldn't want it said that it took less than a full legion of them to bring down Naras of Grey Mountain!"

Ceres stood there, watching the soldiers keep coming, and she knew she had to do something. More than that, there was only one obvious thing to do. She charged.

She blurred into the ranks of the soldiers, cutting left and right in the midst of the strange calm the forest folk had taught her. She spun and thrust with techniques she'd first learned as a combatlord, and, when one of the soldiers tried to grab her, Ceres felt her powers lash out automatically, leaving nothing but stone behind.

"Ceres! Ceres!"

She heard the chanting of the crowd start as she fought. She ducked a sword stroke and cut out at ankle height, then leapt high to kick a soldier back into two others. She parried a slash, then grabbed a soldier and threw him with all the strength her blood gave her.

Around her, Ceres saw the combatlords fighting for their lives. They had no armor, and none of the discipline of the soldiers, but each one was already starting to cut down foes. Ceres saw the bearded one swinging his axe in arcs that left crimson trails of blood behind, while another whirled a spear, darting it past shields into the ranks of those behind them.

Each of them fought like ten men or more, but to Ceres even the combatlords looked slow. She cut through Lucious's troops as easily as some noble lady taking a stroll through a garden, plucking blooms as she went. She leaned back from a sword cut, sliced through an enemy's arm, and then unleashed a burst of killing force that flung soldiers back from her.

"Ceres! Ceres!"

For a moment, Ceres had space to think, and she could hear the crowd truly cheering her now. But cheering her wasn't enough. Eventually, this many soldiers might bring even her down, but they couldn't bring down the whole crowd.

"Stop sitting there and watching," Cere yelled above the clash of metal on metal. "If you want to be free, you can't leave it to someone else! You have to fight for yourselves!" She dodged a charge, cutting a soldier across the back. "Fight now! Take your destiny in your own hands!"

Ceres fought, and even with all the times she'd fought before, this one felt different. The powers within her seemed to pulse in harmony with her every movement. She cut and fought with speed and strength greater than anything she could have imagined before, yet it still felt as though she was simply fitting into the way things needed to be, exactly as she'd been taught. She knew without having to think exactly where to put her blades next, keeping moving, never stopping in one place for long.

More soldiers tried to grab her, and again her powers lashed out, leaving statues where there had been men before. That worried Ceres, because it had been that legacy of her bloodline that had drained so much from her before.

Yet for now, at least, Ceres felt as alive, and as strong, as she'd ever felt. She caught a sword between her two crossed blades, drew them back across the throat of another enemy, then thrust to either

112

side to bring more down. It seemed that everywhere she turned, there was flesh to cut, the threat of blades to deflect, or the presence of Lucious's soldiers to avoid.

At the thought of Lucious, Ceres looked up to the royal balcony. She could still see him there, looking down on the fight as he watched the bloodshed, except now, his glee at the violence seemed to have given way to worry, even fear.

"Good," Ceres said to herself as she continued to fight. Lucious deserved to be scared. If Ceres could get close to him, she would make sure it was the last thing he ever felt.

She continued to whirl, striking and defending faster than she could have managed before her powers came to her, cutting a clear space among the soldiers who surrounded her. She dodged between the stone forms of the soldiers who had tried to grab her, using them as a kind of ring of stone fortifications to defend. Bodies piled up around her, and still Ceres fought.

She saw the other combatlords continuing to fight around her, each standing at the center of his own pile of bodies, yet none of them seemed to be dancing through his foes the way Ceres was, and several seemed to be slowing. Even as Ceres watched, she saw a large man who fought with spiked gloves fall beneath the blades of a dozen men.

Another combatlord stumbled over the body of a soldier, going down. Another soldier stood over him, lifting a sword. Ceres threw out a hand automatically, and her powers jerked his blade away. The combatlord rolled, coming up to his feet in time to stab the soldier through the stomach.

"Combatlords, to me!" Ceres yelled, knowing that she had to take control of this. The combatlords were incredible fighters, but they didn't know how to work together. Ceres stood within the circle of stone figures she'd created, cutting down any soldiers who came near while the combatlords looked her way.

They seemed to understand what she intended, because they fought their way into the circle of stone figures she'd created, defending it the way they might have defended a fortress. Protected by stone like that, the soldiers couldn't surround them or come at them more than one at a time. They could fight, and they could win.

More than that, Ceres saw fights starting to break out in the stands as the spectators started to grab for the guards there to control them. She saw one group pull down a guard, dragging his weapons from him while they lashed out with their fists. She saw another guard cut down a woman, only for three more to take her place, knocking him from the stands.

Ceres could feel the energy of the revolt growing in that moment, and she knew that in a matter of minutes it would burst from the Stade. All the attempts to declare the rebellion done would count for nothing in the face of this fresh outpouring of popular anger. The crowds would go from the Stade and pour out into the streets to take the city.

It was a thought to make satisfaction sit deep in Ceres. It was the kind of uprising Anka might have been proud of. It was the kind of thing Sartes and their father would have wanted. Maybe they were already fighting up there, helping where they could.

Ceres couldn't know that for certain, though. She couldn't do anything but parry the next blade, deal with the next soldier, and try to hold her section of the makeshift fortress her powers had built on the floor of the Stade.

No matter how well they fought, the soldiers were still between them and the exit. There was no way out, and the armored warriors of the Empire just kept coming.

CHAPTER TWENTY FOUR

Stephania barely held her disgust in check as she made her way through the poorest areas of Delos, through the twisting streets of the Tangled quarter, yet there was an upside to it. It was a reminder of just how much she had, just how much there was for her to fight for.

It was the same thing she felt every time she had to go out into the city to meet an informant herself or stock up on the kinds of things she couldn't leave to her handmaidens. The world outside the palace was brutal and dirty, and that was all the more reason for Stephania to ensure that she kept her place.

There were some things worth taking risks for, though. Not love—she'd learned that the hard way. Hate, though, revenge, would always be worth the effort.

"Keep watching for trouble," Stephania told her handmaiden as they made their way along winding streets that stank of too much humanity in too small a space.

"Yes, my lady," the girl replied.

Stephania sighed. What was the point of wrapping up in cloaks to disguise themselves if the stupid girl insisted on advertising who they were every time she spoke? Perhaps she should have brought Elethe with her after all. At least her new senior handmaiden knew what she was supposed to do in circumstances more demanding than seducing a minor noble or listening at doorways. Worse, the girl seemed to have no sense of direction. They'd been looking for the witch they sought for an hour now.

Stephania didn't like the feel of the city today. She'd been sure, in the wake of the peace declaration, that the city would be quiet, and it was, but there were different kinds of quiet in the world. She knew the difference between someone pretending to sleep and someone in the depth of dreams. She knew the difference between an empty room and one where someone was merely hiding. This felt like all of that, but it felt like more.

It felt like the quiet that came when a hawk was flying over a forest, looking for prey.

"Be ready," Stephania whispered.

"Yes, my—"

They stepped out of an alley: two rough-looking men and a young woman who wasn't much better. All wore rags. The two men held knives. How could anyone let themselves get like that?

"Look at them," the young woman said. "Trying to hide under cloaks so rich either one could buy food for a month."

"Don't you know that there's a rebellion going on?" one of the men asked. "Bad things happen to nobles out on the streets."

"Bad things," the other agreed.

Stephania pushed back her hood. "Do you happen to know a witch who lives around here?" she asked, as easily as if they'd been chatting over spiced wine.

"Listen to her, asking about Old Hara as if they're friends," the young woman said in a mocking tone.

Stephania reached into her cloak. She brought out a coin pouch with the faintest of nods to her handmaiden. It was time to see if the girl had any worth at all.

"I can pay you for the information," Stephania said.

"Oh, we'll take that," one of the men replied, stepping forward. He struck Stephania then, and she tasted blood. "That, and everything else you have."

Stephania's hand darted into her cloak, and the man gasped as a knife took him in the chest. She stepped back to let him fall, and saw her handmaiden struggling with the other. She cut his throat from behind, not caring that the blood went over her servant. It was a lot easier than it had been the first time she stabbed someone. That was interesting to note.

"Now," Stephania said, turning to the young woman who'd accompanied the men, "you were going to tell us where to find this 'Old Hara.'"

Stephania could see the fear there. Good, she could trust fear.

"T-turn left where you see the sign of three coins," the woman said. "She lives in the house with the stone snake above the door."

"Thank you," Stephania said. She turned to her handmaiden. "Do you think you can kill *this* one yourself, or must I do it too?"

Stephania didn't bother watching while her handmaiden did what was required. The girl caught her up quickly enough, wiping away some of the blood while Stephania was just approaching the witch's home.

Why did those with knowledge or power live in places like this? The house looked hunched in, set between two larger tenements that appeared ready to fall on it at any moment. The door jamb did indeed have a stone snake carved into it, staring down as though it might bite any unwanted visitors.

Stephania pushed at the door, then ducked on instinct as a pair of red-eyed crows flew out, their claws shining in the sunlight.

"Don't let them scratch you, Lady Stephania," a voice called from inside. "They've been stepping about in some of my rarer poisons."

Stephania didn't ask how the woman knew who she was. True witches had ways of knowing these things, although they rarely had much to do with magic. Probably the woman had seen her coming.

"Do come in," the witch called. "If you've come this far to see me, I imagine we have a lot to discuss."

Stephania went into the woman's home, and the interior wasn't much better than the outside. Clutter filled shelves on every wall. Skulls sat next to jars filled with preserved insects. Books sat open on benches. The scent of the place mixed dung with the acrid smells of alchemy, rare blooms with burning.

A large iron pot hung over a hearth at one end of the main room. The woman who stood in front of it wasn't as old as Stephania had guessed she would be. Probably no more than forty or so. She had a few streaks of gray in her hair, the barest hints of wrinkles around her eyes. Those eyes had a look in them that said they'd seen more than most though, and there was something cruel about her smile.

"It's rare that I have royalty come to visit me," Old Hara said. She gestured to the iron pot. "And you've brought the help. How nice. Can I tempt you to a little something to eat, my dears?"

Stephania looked at the pot and didn't want to think about all the things that might have been cooked up in it. Even now, the scent coming off it was nauseating.

"It wasn't tales of your culinary skills that brought me here," Stephania said.

"No?" That nasty smile was back. "Then what, my darlings? I have powders, potions, and poisons for any occasion. A little late for a maiden's helper or a love potion, I suspect, and I'm sure the physicians at the castle can deal with most of the other problems a noble lady might run into. Something to deal with a rival, perhaps? A nice tincture of arsenic, or a dose of feralwort to slip into someone's tea?"

"Feralwort is a joke that playwrights put in because they don't know any better," Stephania shot back. "You can smell it at a dozen yards, taste it in anything other than the strongest spices, and in the time it takes to work, I could craft an antidote twice over. If you're offering me *that,* I doubt I've come to the right place."

"You'd be amazed at how many gullible nobles buy it from me," Old Hara said. "I make a good deal of coin from them. I'm not sure if half of them even use it. They just keep it around so they can seem dangerous. I guess there's more than *seeming* to you though, lady."

Stephania's smile was a lot tighter than the older woman's. "One look at my companion could tell you that. So far, you've given me offers of hedge-witch stuff, most of which I could brew myself. Including better poisons than feralwort."

Stephania meant that as a warning. She didn't like having her time wasted, and often, the kind of people who sold poisons couldn't be trusted.

"Then what can I provide you with, my lady?" Old Hara asked. "If you can craft your own poisons so easily, why come to visit a poor old woman with a talent for forgotten things?"

"For information," Stephania said. She pulled out the gold she'd been going to offer to their would-be attackers. "Expensive information."

"Hmm... I'd have thought it would be me telling you that. If you're opening with it, it must be *very* expensive information. So what exactly is it that's so important to you?"

Stephania had been thinking about the best way to put it since she left the palace. Ultimately, though, there were times when it was necessary to be direct.

"I want to know the best way to kill one of the Ancient Ones."

She saw Old Hara's smile fade, her expression hardening. There was something about the change that told her she'd come to the right place, there among the oddments and the potions. This woman knew something, and Stephania would find it out, whatever it took.

"This is about the girl who bested Prince Lucious's combatlord?" Old Hara said. "A girl who could turn a man to stone, and who could bring an army with the talk of her bloodline."

Stephania wasn't going to be impressed just because the other woman had listened to a few rumors.

"Ceres," Stephania said. "Her name is Ceres. She has taken too much from me. Now it's time for her to pay."

"I had heard that she was captured," the witch said.

"She escaped. There are soldiers turned to stone in the cell where she was held." Stephania couldn't help thinking of the obvious then. What if it had been her? What if she'd been touching the peasant when her powers had lashed out like that? *Her* powers? It was no more than an accident of blood, but somehow it meant that they were all meant to bow down to her. Well, Stephania wouldn't allow that.

She could see the witch considering, as if she had a choice about talking to Stephania. If necessary, Stephania would have what she want tortured from her. It was dangerous to tangle with her kind though. Better to do this a more civilized way.

"If you know anything, I need your help," Stephania said, trying to put as much pleading into her voice as possible.

Still, the old witch looked thoughtful, working her hands against one another as if washing them. "It's a dangerous path you're contemplating walking," she said. "I have information that might lead you to what you want to know, but I've a piece of advice first. Turn around. Go back to your palace. You'll be happier. There are some roads where, once you start on them, it's hard to turn back."

Perhaps there were, but Stephania suspected that they were worth the effort anyway.

"I came here for answers," she said.

"Answers are expensive," Old Hara replied. "More expensive than coin, because giving them buys me trouble with people it's better not to cross."

Stephania put her coin pouch back beneath her cloak. "What then?"

She saw the witch shrug. "There are rituals, potions... research that needs special ingredients. The smugglers bring me a lot, but even so, time is catching up with me."

"What do you want?" Stephania repeated.

"There are rituals that call for the blood of a healthy younger woman, her skin, her bones." Stephania saw her nod toward the handmaiden. "If you really want to know, then I'll take *her*."

Stephania's impulse was to tell the woman no. To torture the information from her as she'd planned. She had loyalty from her handmaidens because she protected them in return. This wasn't the kind of thing she did.

"My lady?" the girl said, in that annoying voice of hers that had got them into so much trouble in the street.

The truth was that the girl had been less than useless so far. Now the only question was how badly Stephania wanted to know how to defeat Ceres. How much did she want her revenge?

There was only one answer to that.

"Take her," Stephania said. "She let me be *struck*."

The girl raised her hands as if to ward off a threat, but she didn't seem to have words to go with it at first. When they came, it was little more than a babble.

"My lady… please, I can do better… you can't do this…"

Stephania saw Old Hara approach the handmaiden, lifting a hand and then blowing across it almost as if blowing a kiss. Stephania saw the golden spray of powder that caught the girl in the face as she gasped.

She collapsed a moment later, while the witch dusted off her hands.

"Goldbreath," Stephania said with a certain amount of awe. The poison was a rarity, distilled from the ground stems of flowers brought in from the Southlands.

"I had it ready in case you were foolish enough to attack me," she said to Stephania. "I'm impressed that you recognized it."

"I have done my part," Stephania said. "What you have to tell me had better be worth it. How do I stop an Ancient One?"

"You don't."

Anger rose in Stephania then, and she reached into her cloak.

"But there is one who can," the witch went on quickly. "A sorcerer who has spent his life studying their works. I have seen him kill one with his own hands."

"Where do I find this sorcerer?" Stephania demanded.

"In the lands of Felldust," the witch replied. "where the falling sun meets the skulls of the stone dead."

"And what does that mean?" Stephania asked.

She saw the witch spread her hands. "It is what I was told in case I ever needed to find him. It should be simple enough, for one with your resources, and if you say I sent you, he might even keep from taking your mind from you and reducing you to his servant. I'll say again though, this is a dangerous business. Is your anger worth the risk?"

Anger alone wouldn't be. Stephania was used to being cold with her anger, pushing it down. Revenge, though, was always worth it.

"That is not your business," Stephania said. "Tell me, if I'd killed you after learning what I wanted, what signal would you not have given me for the sorcerer?"

She saw Old Hara smile again. "A raven sent to him with my mark. You have the cunning to learn the craft, my lady."

It was probably supposed to be a compliment, but Stephania had far better things to learn. She walked away, leaving her handmaiden to her fate.

It was time for vengeance.

CHAPTER TWENTY FIVE

Lucious was anything but happy to be walking away from the Stade and back toward the castle. He had been so eager to watch the final demise of the slaves.

It seemed he didn't have a choice, however.

"You're sure that this couldn't have waited?" Lucious demanded of one of the men. He wore the gilt-edged armor of the royal bodyguard, not the common red and silver of the guards.

"The king said 'at once,' your highness," the man said, with a flatness that reminded Lucious of teak or stone.

"And did he say what this was about?" Lucious demanded, as they continued to hurry toward the castle.

Beside him, the silence was palpable. The royal bodyguard didn't so much as dignify the request with an answer. If Lucious could have done it, he would have had the man demoted for that, or sent to the fringes of the Empire to fight the raiders who sometimes came over the border, but these guards answered only to the king.

The walk to the castle did little to improve Lucious's mood. It wasn't just the fractiousness in the city, when everyone should have been staying in their homes, afraid of him. It was the way he had to walk between the two guards to keep the threats of the streets away, looking less like a figure they were protecting than a prisoner for them to guard.

By the time they reached the castle, and the doors to his father's chambers, Lucious was fuming. When one of the bodyguards there stepped into his path, Lucious almost struck the man. Only the thought that he was probably more than capable of beating Lucious to a pulp slowed him.

"Get out of my way, man!" Lucious ordered.

"Forgive me, your highness, but you are still wearing your sword."

Lucious wanted to draw it and thrust it through the man, but instead, he handed it over with bad grace, throwing in his dagger just to make the point. The guards finally stepped back, and Lucious stepped past them.

"Remember that one day I will be your king," Lucious said in what he hoped was a suitably dangerous tone. Again, he met silence.

His father was sitting on the throne he kept within his chambers, of course. He always did when he wanted to appear serious. Lucious would have believed it better if he hadn't known of all the serving girls he'd had "attend" him there on that throne, and all the times he'd gotten so drunk he'd fallen off it. Both traditions Lucious fully intended to continue when he was king.

Today, his father's expression was serious, even stern. There was no sign of Lucious's mother. After the last time they'd spoken here, Lucious had the sense to bow deeply, even if he felt that his father ought to be the one rising to meet him.

"Lucious, my son," his father said, standing. "I expected you sooner."

"I was busy dealing with things in the Stade. Securing *our* Empire," Lucious said. "Doing all the things you wanted me to do."

"The things I wanted you to do, yes," his father said. He walked into the area of the chambers where the statues of long dead kings looked down. Lucious followed, even though he hated the dead eyes staring down at him.

"Do you remember the lessons Cosmas drilled into you?" his father asked. "Do you know who these men are?"

"My ancestors," Lucious answered, because really, who had time to remember the names of the dead?

"Your ancestors, yes," his father said. "Some of them were good men. Some of them were bloody-handed tyrants. This is Nemius, the Year Long King. They say he was a wise and good man who tried to change the Empire."

"He sounds more like a fool to me," Lucious said. "Why call him the Year Long King?"

"He died in less than a year, trying to help with the bubbling plague," his father said. "As you'd know if you'd learned your history."

"Did you really call me here to discuss ancestors so stupid they couldn't keep away from plague pits?" Lucious demanded.

He heard his father sigh in the way that had always annoyed Lucious, as though Lucious only existed to disappoint him.

"You have no patience, Lucious. It is just one of your problems."

Lucious thought he'd had plenty of patience, waiting for his time to rule, but he didn't say that. Instead, he laughed.

"And what good did patience do your Year Long King?" he asked. "Probably, if he'd had less, he would have gotten more done."

"Do you have any respect for the achievements of the men before you?" his father demanded. "Do you have any respect for *anything*?"

"I have respect for power," Lucious said. "For the strength of our arms and the position our blood gives us. Does it help me to know about dead men?"

"It might help you to avoid some of their faults," his father snapped back.

Lucious doubted it. He pointed to one at random, since they were all the same to him. "What about this one?"

"Phenus," his father replied. "He fought wars to expand the Empire. He also taxed his peasants too heavily, and endured years of famine." He moved over to another. "This is Falkon the Slaver, who took the daughters of his nobles to his bed, and was poisoned by his own courtiers. This is—"

"Are you going to go through all of them?" Lucious demanded.

He shrank back as his father rounded on him. Damn him for always being able to make him feel fear, despite his age.

"You are not listening, Lucious. These are men who went too far, as you do! You have terrorized Delos and the countryside around it. You have taken and taken, with no thought for what is left behind. You have been cruel for the sake of being cruel, and only fueled the rebellion!"

"I have done nothing you did not tell me to," Lucious pointed out. "You told me that nobles could take what they wanted from peasants, so I did. You told me to remind them of their place, so I did."

"But I forgot that *we* have a place too," his father replied. "I am not just blaming you, my son. I forgot as much as you did that we exist to look after the Empire, not just to take from it. A shepherd who cares for his flock year after year, not the wolves who descend upon it to slaughter it."

"That sounds like the kind of nonsense Lord West might have said," Lucious countered. He was glad that the old fool was dead, although it rankled that he'd died clean. A traitor like that didn't deserve it.

"Lord West was one of my closest friends," his father said, sounding older than ever to Lucious. "He was an honorable man. You were going to kill him as though he was there for your entertainment."

"I was going to make an example that would stop others," Lucious retorted, anger running through him with every beat of his heart. "Don't start moralizing, Father. You have done plenty of cruel things in your time, and you had your part in this. You *wanted* this."

His father turned to look him in the eye. "And now, I do not."

He said it as though it were that easy. As though the world turned according to his whim. As though Lucious was supposed to change who he was, simply because his father no longer wanted what he once had.

"I have been issuing orders today," his father said. "I have commanded that the captured rebels should be released. The taxes will be put back to their previous levels, and there will be no more seizures of goods or random tortures. This stops, Lucious."

Lucious froze, hardly believing what he was hearing.

"And how does looking weak help us?" Lucious demanded.

"It is not weak to show restraint, or to do what is right," the king said. "Although it has taken me a long time to remember that, and I am not sure I taught it to you at all."

Because it *wasn't* true, Lucious thought. It was simply a lie told by the weak to try to rein in the strong. He'd thought his father knew better.

"And that is why I have something else to tell you, Lucious," his father said. "Something I must admit to the world."

A heavy silence fell, until he finally looked him in the eye with grave solemnity.

"Thanos…he is your brother."

He said it as though it was some great revelation, and Lucious had to remind himself that he wasn't supposed to know the secret of his brother's parentage. Thankfully, his father was too caught up in his own confession to notice the slip.

"I was young, and I was foolish," King Claudius went on. "But I was stupider to try to cover up what happened. I had the events stricken from the records, but I have already sent to have that put right. I will reinstate Thanos as my son."

That caught Lucious by surprise, stealing his breath from him. He felt his world spinning out from beneath his feet.

"No," he said softly. "No, this can't—"

"It's true," his father assured him, as though that was what Lucious was worried about. "Thanos is your brother."

"I know that!" Lucious yelled back. "Of course I know that! And he knows that, and probably half the rebellion knows that by now! Do you think that this charade fooled anyone?"

His father looked stunned.

125

"Don't raise your voice to me, boy," the king said. "I am still your father."

"And that of who knows how many other brats," Lucious said. "We all take our turns with the peasants, but that doesn't mean we have to acknowledge their whelps!"

His father turned red.

"Thanos's mother was no peasant!" his father snapped back, and for a moment, Lucious thought that he might strike him. Lucious found himself taking a step back automatically, and hated himself for it.

"I will not accept this," Lucious said, with his fists clenched. "I will not. *I* am your son. My mother is your wife!"

"All of that is true," his father said, and there was something in his tone that made Lucious think that perhaps he regretted it all. That made anger sit in Lucious's chest like a stone, the weight of it making it hard to breathe.

"Is that all you have to say?" Lucious demanded. "Just that it's true that I'm your son, my mother is your wife? Make it sound like it means something, you old fool."

"I *have* been a fool," his father said. "A fool to think that you would understand this, Lucious. I have spent my life being blind to what you are. I made excuses for you, when I should have taught you better. I set you the worst kind of example, and you followed it."

Lucious didn't say anything then. He wasn't sure what there was left to say.

"This will take time to adjust to, for you and Athena, I know," his father said, "but you *will* get used to the idea, Lucious." His father reached out to touch the statue that represented Lucious's grandfather. "You must, because when I acknowledge Thanos, he will be my oldest son. My heir. He will be your king one day, Lucious."

Lucious shook his head, refusing to accept what he was hearing.

"He's a traitor. He helped the rebellion, and you reward him like this?"

"He is a man willing to risk everything for what he believes to be right," his father said. "The Empire needs a ruler with that kind of honor."

Lucious felt as though he could have been one of the statues around him, as cold and empty as any of them. He'd passed beyond simple anger now, into something blank and dangerous and pure.

Perhaps if his father hadn't touched him in that moment, it might still have been all right. Lucious had swallowed his anger before, many times. He'd pushed it back, held himself back. Then again, where had that ever gotten him?

As it was, his father was stupid enough to reach out and touch his shoulder, as if that would be enough to pacify him. As if affection from the man who had just ruined his life would make things better.

Lucious lashed out on instinct, feeling his fist sink deep into his father's stomach. It felt good to finally do it when he'd dreamed about it so many times. So good, in fact, that he did it again.

"Lucious," his father said, "what are you doing? Stop this."

The best part of it, the part Lucious suspected would stay with him until the day he died, was the fear he heard there. The fear he'd always wanted to hear from his father. The same fear he'd somehow managed to inspire in Lucious all his life. Lucious felt as though he was watching it from afar, enjoying it the way he might have enjoyed a particularly brutal performance in the Stade.

It was from that point of view that he saw himself lifting the stone bust of the Year Long King. It seemed appropriate, somehow, using the bust of one royal fool on another, a king who had reigned barely long enough to cut short one who had reigned far too long.

"Lucious," his father begged. "Don't!"

Lucious struck, and the feeling of it wasn't what he expected. He'd anticipated that it would feel spectacular, like lying with a bevy of maidens or slaughtering his way through a village. Instead, like so many of the moments in his life he'd looked forward to, it felt like nothing at all. Nothing beyond the crunch of stone against skull, at least, the dull, thudding impact of it all.

Lucious struck him again anyway, just to see if he would feel anything then.

Still nothing.

Standing over his father, he knew he should have felt guilt, or shame or one of the other emotions that peasants seemed to feel so strongly.

Mostly, he felt satisfaction.

Satisfaction, and a sense that this was all his father's fault. Standing there like that, watching what were surely his father's last breaths, he couldn't think of anything but the stupidity of the man. He'd been doing the right things. He'd given Lucious the chance to do as he wished. Lucious had even believed that in time he would be proud of all that his son had done to secure the Empire.

Instead, he'd proven himself as weak and as foolish as all the rest of them. Lucious let the statue fall from his hand, taking care to wipe away the blood. No doubt the royal bodyguard would try to kill him if they saw him like this, yet once his father was dead, he would be king, and they wouldn't so much as raise a hand.

"Lucious..." his father breathed from the floor, breathing his dying breath.

Lucious scowled down.

"That's *King* Lucious," he replied, as he headed for the door.

CHAPTER TWENTY SIX

Thanos crept through the castle, looking around with every step for the guards who might be waiting. He couldn't let himself be captured before he made his offer to his father.

He pressed himself into a niche behind a drape as guards walked past, not daring to breathe as footsteps echoed in front of his hiding place. He held still until he was sure that the threat was gone, then continued on his way.

He knew the secret paths through the castle as well as anyone. He'd run through the halls and the passages as a child, learning every hiding place, dodging his tutors or playing with the other children of the castle when no one was around to tell him he couldn't. It served him well now, letting him get closer and closer to his destination.

There was no way to sneak into the royal chambers unobserved, though. Kings with secret passages into their rooms didn't last long, and there were bodyguards on the door, looking as implacable as ever. Thanos thought about distracting them, luring them away, or even just appealing to their loyalty, but he knew better than to try it.

The royal bodyguards knew their tasks, and they were absolutely committed to the king's safety. Perhaps it was because they knew that they would be executed if anything happened to their royal charge. No, there was only one way past them.

Thanos crept as close as he could, and then charged.

He caught the first man with a punch to the jaw that sent him crashing to the ground, then cannoned into the second, grabbing him and dragging him down with him. The man was strong, but Thanos had trained with the best of the combatlords, and he came up on top. He wrapped an arm around the man's throat, squeezing tight. The guard scrabbled for his weapon, but Thanos caught his arm and kept squeezing until his foe went limp.

He let go and tried the door, opening it as quietly as he could.

"Father?"

The room beyond looked set to receive visitors, but it seemed empty. For a moment, Thanos thought that he'd misjudged where his father would be at this time of day, but if the king wasn't in his throne room or out hunting, this was the most likely place for him.

Then Thanos looked beyond the throne.

His heart collapsed.

"No," he said aloud. "It can't be."

His father lay on the floor, his royal robes stained dark with blood. His head looked like a bloody mess, while one of the statuettes from the collection representing previous kings lay on the floor beside him, reddened at the base.

"No!" Thanos cried.

He rushed forward and knelt in the blood that pooled on the floor of his father's rooms, not caring that it soaked into his clothes and covered his hands.

He cradled his father's head, and the king seemed so light then, so fragile that he could have been a child. Thanos felt tears rising to his eyes in a way he might never have thought possible for a man who had been this cruel throughout his life, yet the fact remained that this was his father who lay dead there among the statues of his forebears.

Except that, even as Thanos knelt there beside him, he saw the faint, fluttering rise and fall of his father's chest. He was breathing, if only barely, and even that fact was enough to make hope spring up in Thanos's heart.

When King Claudius' eyes flickered open, Thanos dared to think that things might be all right after all.

"Father, can you hear me?" Thanos asked. "Hold on, it will be all right. I'll fetch help."

"It's too late," the king replied, in between ragged breaths. "I'm… dying, Thanos. I can… feel it."

"No," Thanos insisted. "You can't know that. You've seen men on the battlefield who thought they were going to die and lived. Let me fetch the royal physician."

"I've seen more who… died when they were told they'd live," his father said. "Lucious… has killed me."

"Lucious," Thanos repeated.

The need for retribution, for some kind of justice, burned up in him then. He'd let Lucious get away with so many things, had spared him because of who he was, or how much trouble it would cause.

"I'll kill him for this. I'll tear the castle apart if I have to."

"Thanos, listen to me," his father said. "We don't have… much time."

For the first time, the reality of that hit home. These were the last moments he would ever have with his father. If there had ever been a chance for them to be reconciled, for things to be better, it had been snatched away from them.

"Father," Thanos began, but attempting it then seemed wrong somehow. He'd come there to beg for Stephania's life. The king cut him off in any case.

"Thanos... there are... things I have to tell you. I was foolish." For a moment, his father closed his eyes, and Thanos thought that the end had come, but somehow he kept going. There was a hint of the old strength there when his father spoke again. "When it came to your mother, I was a fool and more than that. I was cruel. I put politics ahead of what I felt. We needed the lands that Athena brought with her, and your mother... it would have made things difficult."

Thanos had heard that part, but he guessed that his father wanted to at least try to make things right.

"It doesn't matter now," Thanos said.

"It matters more than ever," his father replied. "I tried to have you reinstated, but Lucious won't allow that now. He will prevent it, cover up the truth. You will need to be able to prove the truth of it, the whole truth. That means..." His breath caught, hacking as he fought for life.

"What is it, Father?" Thanos asked.

"Father, I like hearing you call me that," the king managed. A look of pain flashed across his face, and Thanos saw him pale. "Felldust. You'll find the answers you need in Felldust. That's where she went after I—"

He gasped again then, his eyes staring up at something beyond Thanos.

"Hold on," Thanos said. "I'll get help. The physicians must be able to do *something*."

There was no answer, though. Thanos had seen enough death already in his life to recognize the moment when the glassy stare of eyes stopped looking at this world.

He reached out almost automatically to shut his father's eyes.

He didn't expect grief in that moment. This was the man, after all, who had terrorized his own empire, who had given Lucious the freedom to do what he wanted and who had put down challenges to his rule with hands as bloody as Thanos's were right then. This was the man who had tried to rule over his life, who had sent him to Haylon, and who had declared Thanos a traitor for his role in helping the rebellion.

He shouldn't have felt anything for this man, but he did. He found deep emptiness welling up in him, in sadness not just for the loss of a father, but the loss of what could have been. He could have had a real father, but he'd never had that. The Empire could have had a king who cared for it. Thanos could have found himself in a position to respect and love his father, rather than seeing him as the symbol of everything cruel and harsh about the way the Empire ruled.

Thanos grieved for that, and also for the fact that he'd never had the chance to know his father *as* his father, only as the king giving him orders that hurt so many. He grieved for the man his father could have been, a man he'd seen in only the briefest of glimpses.

He knelt there in his father's blood, and he felt his tears starting to fall. Thanos wiped them away, but that only left blood on his face, the heat of the smears there cut through by fresh tear tracks. He wiped it away with his sleeves, but that only left Thanos's clothes red.

He stood, not knowing what to do next. Not knowing where to even begin. He'd come there to save Stephania, and instead, he'd found *this*. But what could he do now? Should he sneak away as though nothing had happened? Should he try to get to Stephania and get her out of there safely? Should he do what every bone in his body was aching for him to do, and hunt down Lucious, gutting him for what he'd done to their father?

Should he stay there, simply because he couldn't abandon his father's body?

Thanos didn't know which to do. He couldn't think then, couldn't do anything but feel. He stood there, looking at his still bloody hands, and none of it seemed to make sense.

He wasn't sure how long he stood there, because even the passing of his heartbeats didn't seem to have any meaning then except to draw attention to the fact that his father's heart no longer did.

He was still standing there when he heard the doors to the chambers opening, and he spun round, ready to fight. Some instinct told him that this might be Lucious, and if it was, then Thanos intended to make sure that he didn't leave this room again.

It wasn't Lucious, though.

Guards stood there, more than a dozen fanning out around the edge of the room in a grim circle. The two Thanos had knocked out stood groggily with them, looking as though they had only just been shaken back into consciousness.

Queen Athena stood at their heart, her expression set, looking like some cruel painting of an avenging goddess. Thanos saw her looking over the room, and him, and her dead husband, taking it all in. He saw her gasp, and stumble slightly as she took it all in, her mask of impassive perfection slipping for a moment as she did it.

Thanos saw grief and horror underneath, and some part of him thought better of the queen for it. He hadn't thought that she was capable of feeling anything for others.

"You!" she snarled, her gaze fixing on him. "What have you done? What have you *done*?"

A guard rushed past Thanos, going to the body of the king and bending down over him.

"He's dead!" the man called. "The king is dead."

Two guards drew their swords then, moving to the royal bodyguards Thanos had knocked down. Before the men could move to stop them, the guards' swords slid into their throats and out again, leaving the bodyguards clutching at the wounds as they fell.

Thanos recoiled in horror from the sight of that, and the casual way these men could kill their own for failing. He felt guilty too, because if he hadn't fought his way past the guards, they might still be alive now. Maybe not, though, because they might still have been killed when they found out what Lucious had done.

"You, killed him," Queen Athena said, staring at Thanos. "You killed my husband!"

It occurred to Thanos then what this had to look like. He'd sneaked into the castle, and fought his way past the guards at the door to the royal chambers. Now, the king lay dead behind him, and Thanos was standing there, so covered in his blood that he probably looked like a madman or a monster. If Thanos had found someone else like this, what would *he* have thought?

Even so, Thanos tried to explain the truth of it.

"Lucious did this," he said. "Lucious killed the king because King Claudius was going to undo Lucious's violence and place him second in line to the throne to me."

Even as he said it, Thanos could see the disbelief on every face there. Every face, except that of the queen. For her, there seemed to be a kind of horrified recognition of the truth of it, knowing that it was exactly the kind of thing that her son might do.

"Why would he do such a thing?" Queen Athena demanded.

"Because I'm his son," Thanos replied, and he saw the truth of it register with the queen. "You know what's happening. You know Lucious did this."

"I know no such thing!" Queen Athena bellowed, and Thanos could see her trying to cover her reaction. "You're the one standing there covered in my husband's blood. You're the one who joined up with the rebellion. That's what this is! A last-ditch attempt by them to derail the Empire's victory! Why is no one grabbing that traitor?"

They surged forward for him then, and Thanos fought, because he could see that no one was going to listen to him there. He threw a punch that caught a guard hard in the side, then stepped between two more, making for the door. Unarmed, he couldn't hope to fight so many men. He could only hope to escape.

He ran for the door, but hands grabbed at him. Thanos spun, feeling his elbow connect with a guard's head, but blows rained down on him in return. Guards struck at him from all angles, and if there had only been one or two, then perhaps he might have been able to endure it, even fighting back.

As it was, there were simply too many of them. A pair of guards tackled him, and Thanos went down under a sprawling mass of bodies, with only the fact that the guards were getting in one another's way stopping Thanos from being stomped to death.

Eventually, he felt hands clamping around his arms, dragging him up to his feet and holding him in place in spite of his efforts to get away. He saw Queen Athena watching him with hard-edged hatred that seemed to have an edge of calculation to it.

Thanos could guess what she was thinking. That if it came to a choice between her son and a man who hated the system that had given her so much, there was no choice. That this could be an opportunity as well as a loss. That only one thing would give her control over a son in charge of the Empire.

"You have always hated us," she said, "but I never thought even you would do something so evil. You betrayed your empire, but I never thought you would be so mad as to murder your king!"

"Lucious will betray you in time," Thanos said. "If he can do this to his father, do you really think you're safe?"

Queen Athena stepped forward and struck him hard across the cheek.

"Take this traitor away and execute him," she said.

The last thing Thanos saw was a mound of bodies, pummeling him, dragging him away, smothering out the light as his world went black.

CHAPTER TWENTY SEVEN

From a shadowed doorway Stephania stared out at the ships across the dock, unable to push away the memories of everything that had happened the last time she'd been there. Anger rose at the thought of Thanos's abandonment of her, and the cold hardness of it was more than enough to push away her fear.

She was afraid because of what might happen if Lucious found out that she was trying to leave Delos. So many of her old informants were his now that she didn't know who to trust. If he found out about this, he probably *would* keep her under lock and key, forcing her to do his bidding.

Or try, anyway. Stephania would see him dead before that.

Which would be as good as suicide, Stephania thought, wrapping her cloak tighter around herself. She tried to tell herself that the reason she was shivering was the cold of the sea air.

She was still trying to make sense of the chaos at the docks. There were too many ships, with too many unfamiliar names. She could have tried for one of the few imperial galleys lined up there, but it would take time to gather together the appropriate blackmail material on one of the captains, and right then, Stephania didn't have time.

There were a lot of things she didn't have. She didn't have her handmaidens, because she'd had to leave them behind at the castle to maintain some pretense of normality. She didn't have her full resources, just three bags containing gold, silver, and gems, almost as carefully hidden as the knives and vials of poison she'd brought. Compared to the advantages being at the heart of the Empire gave her, it was practically nothing.

Stephania could see armed men making their way along the docks now. Rough-looking men; exactly the sort Lucious might employ quietly. Stephania huddled deeper into the stone alcove of the doorway, making sure they hadn't spotted her.

There had to be someone. Some ship that would go where she wanted to and that would take her as a passenger with no questions asked. The *Dantenine*? No, its captain had a reputation for betraying passengers. The *Fire Adder*? That might be heading for her destination, but if Stephania could have bribed its captain so easily, she would have used it for her first escape with Thanos. She'd burned so many bridges trying to save him that she couldn't find one safe to cross now.

It was just one more thing to hate him for now.

As brightest day does turn to night, so love to hate can spin, Stephania thought, trying to remember where the small fragment of poetry was from. It didn't sound like the kind of thing one of her would-be suitors might recite. Ah, that was it; the Ancient One poet Varaleth. Old Cosmas had gotten her to read his works once when—

Stephania shook her head. She was trying to distract herself from the moment when she had to act, when this was a moment that called for decisiveness. She had to remember who she was. It didn't *matter* that she couldn't find the perfect ship. She would find one and make it work, through bribery, or threats, or whatever else it took.

Stephania looked over to the far side of the docks, and that was when she saw the boat that held her handmaiden, Elethe. Stephania had assumed that the girl had either been killed in the course of her task, taken along by Thanos, or had simply decided to tarry too long in the city. Instead, she sat in a small boat, watched by another woman who looked as though she could have been a pirate or a mercenary to Stephania's eye.

Well, that was acceptable. Both were easy enough to bribe, and in the worst-case scenario, where she simply had to poison the woman, at least she would have her handmaiden back to help search for another ship.

Stephania made her way along the dock, tightening her hand on one of her knives beneath her cloak just in case, feeling the hilt of it press deep into the palm of her hand. To her surprise, the woman on the boat looked up as she approached. She hadn't moved as quietly as she'd thought.

On the boat, Stephania saw a flash of recognition mixed with hope cross Elethe's face. It was sweet that despite everything, the girl would still think of her as a savior. If she'd been there with Stephania when they'd visited the old witch, she might have found out how little that counted for.

"My lady," Elethe said.

Stephania snarled to herself. Did *none* of her handmaidens understand the stupidity of that?

"You're Lady Stephania?" the other woman said.

"Just as I promised," Elethe replied. "Thanos has helped her to escape and sent her to us."

Stephania smiled then, because she realized this was one handmaiden capable of seeing more possibilities than most. She'd given Stephania more than enough information to begin with. She put back the hood of her cloak, so that they could get a better view of her. She schooled her features into a perfect image of the frightened escapee, terrified of being caught. It wasn't difficult. She just thought about what would happen to her if Lucious caught up with her.

"Elethe," she said. "Who is this woman? Thanos... he sent me here. He... he said you might help."

She was probably putting it on a little thickly, but Elethe seemed to be happy for the distraction. She rose up behind the other woman in silence, obviously ready to strike.

"Well, you don't need to worry," the woman said. "As soon as Thanos gets here, I'll get us all to safety. Sail you anywhere in the world you want to go."

Stephania hurriedly signaled for Elethe to stop. Just a twitch of the fingers, but it was enough for her handmaiden to sit back down. The other woman there spun as though expecting an attack, but Stephania stepped forward.

"Anywhere? I'm sorry, but I don't even know who you are, not really."

"Lady Stephania," Elethe said. "Can I present to you Captain Felene? She has... many accomplishments, apparently. She's been telling me about a few while we waited."

"Just Felene," the other woman said. "Will Thanos be long?"

Stephania shook her head, remembering to make it look as though she was anguished by all that was happening to her.

"Thanos... won't be coming," she said. "They killed him."

She'd always had the ability to cry on demand. She'd learned it as a girl, as the best method to get her way. Even now, it still had its value, as she felt a tear roll down her cheek.

"So you *do* feel something for him," Felene said.

"You don't get to ask me that," Stephania said.

She saw the boat captain's expression harden. "I do if we're traveling together. If you've just cost Thanos his life."

"Then yes, I feel something for him!" Stephania snapped back. After all, she'd only just told herself that love and hate weren't so far apart. "And yes, he died for me, and I feel awful about it. I wouldn't have let him do it, but he insisted."

She saw Felene nod. "Yes, that's the kind of thing Thanos would do."

Stephania saw the captain's hand tighten on the edge of her boat. Stephania hoped she hadn't gone too far. It would be no use if the woman ran off in some desperate quest to avenge Thanos.

"I hope you know how lucky you are to have known him," Felene said. "He saved me, and I owe him, and now so do you. You owe it to him to make it worth his sacrifice."

"I will," Stephania said, with what she hoped was a suitable level of sincerity. "I will even avenge him, but to do that, there is someone I must find. Someone who can help us against the Empire, even if we must do it secretly. Even if we must pretend we support them."

"Who?" Felene asked, and just by the tone of it, Stephania knew she had her.

"There is a sorcerer, in the land of Felldust," Stephania said. "I think he can help us."

She saw Felene considering, but it wasn't for long. The sailor nodded sharply.

"All right," she said. "Felldust it is. As I told Thanos, I've always wanted to spirit away a princess. We *will* have revenge, though?"

"Absolutely," Stephania said. "I promise you."

It was just a question of on whom. They would go to Felldust, find the sorcerer, and Stephania would have vengeance on Ceres. As for Thanos, if he wasn't actually dead already, she had a way of making sure he ended up that way.

She put a hand on her belly. She couldn't feel the child growing within her yet, but it would come. She would raise her child in full knowledge of its place in the Empire, and she would teach it every skill it needed. She would raise her child with a pure hatred of Thanos that would ensure his death should they ever meet.

"Is everything all right, my lady?" Elethe asked as she helped Stephania to board the boat.

Stephania nodded, and for the first time, smiled widely.

"Everything is exactly as it should be."

CHAPTER TWENTY EIGHT

Ceres felt more like a commander defending a fort than a combatlord in the middle of the Stade right then. The battle seemed to flow in concentric rings around her, and as she cut and thrust, spun and jumped, Ceres felt as though she was the bull's-eye of some giant archer's roundel.

There was the ring of combatlords around her, each fighting with strength of a dozen normal warriors. There was the ring of petrified soldiers, looking like some ancient circle of standing stones, forcing the Empire's soldiers to get through one at a time, pushing and shoving as they worked their way closer to the real fight. Beyond them, there was the wider ring of the crowd, throwing whatever they could find, grabbing weapons from guards and bringing them down with their bare hands where they needed to.

Ceres had no time to observe it, though; she was too busy fighting, rushing from the side of one combatlord to another, cutting and stabbing with both of her blades. She thrust past the guard of one opponent, ducked back behind one of the stone figures as another slashed at her, and cut again.

A crossbow bolt bounced from one of the stone figures there, but no others followed. There were obviously too many soldiers surrounding them to risk firing into the melee. Anyone doing so stood more chance of killing their own men than hitting one of the combatlords.

Even so, Ceres didn't dare pull back into open space. Instead, with the speed and strength her blood gave her, Ceres danced from opponent to opponent, sliding past defenses, avoiding attacks and cutting her attackers down. She threw one back with the full force of the energy that lay within her, slamming him back onto the blades of his fellows, then sliced the head from a spear with crossed blades.

More spears came in between the gaps in their stone ring of protection, searching for flesh like creepers topped by razor sharp leaves. She saw the combatlord with the axe stabbed through the shoulder, bellowing as he wrenched it out and swinging his axe in return.

Ceres wrenched one from the hands of an attacker, passing it to a combatlord to use. The big man thrust with it in one hand, wielding a curved sword with the other to fend off the responses.

There was none of the elegance of the Stade about the fighting. There were simply too many opponents for that. The Stade was a place where the spectacle normally bloomed out of two evenly matched opponents pushing one another to their limits. Here, every opponent who tried to force his way into the stone circle was easy to cut down, but there was always another.

And another after that.

It became a question of fighting as cleanly and efficiently as possible. Even with all the strength her powers gave her, Ceres could feel her arms growing tired with the mechanical repetition of slicing through flesh and knocking away enemies. One of her swords snapped on a shield and Ceres had to drop to one knee to avoid the sword that followed. She stabbed upwards, caught the dying soldier's sword as he released it, then spun to strike a second soldier with both blades.

There was another ring forming around the stone one now, composed of the bodies of the dead, piling one on top of another as more and more soldiers clambered over their fallen comrades to try to break through and be the ones to finally kill Ceres.

Ceres couldn't believe that they just kept coming. Surely there had to come a point where they realized that they weren't going to prevail, and that continuing to charge the ring of stone figures was suicide. Even while they continued to do it, they were being harried by the crowd, but if the soldiers ever turned their full attention to the people there, they would slaughter them. They were simply too well armed.

The only hope was to keep going, but there *was* no hope in that, because no matter how many they killed, there always seemed to be more. Ceres could see the pressure building now, as exhaustion set in among the combatlords. One parried a thrust too late, and grunted as a blade sliced along his arm. Another fell, a spear driving deep into his chest.

Ceres saw the danger at once, rushing to fill the gap. She turned a soldier to stone as he tried to push into the circle, then hacked at the arm of a second who tried to reach through the gap.

Silence fell, no new attackers came, and for a moment, Ceres thought that maybe it was done. She dared to look out through the stones. What she saw there made her duck back hurriedly. Crossbowmen and archers stood at the front of a ring of soldiers, weapons raised.

"Everyone take cover!" Ceres yelled, pressing into the protection of one of the stones.

Arrows and bolts darkened the sky, hanging for a moment before they fell. When they fell, they took their toll. Ceres winced as she saw combatlords falling, peppered with shafts. Most of the arrows missed or struck the stones, but with so many in the air, some had to strike home.

The worst part was that there was nothing she could do to stop it. Ceres had created the shelter that kept some of them safe, but eventually, the rain of arrows would kill them all. They could charge out into the space beyond, but that would just make them better targets. They couldn't even help the people in the stands, who were still fighting bravely, but who were slowly being pushed back by the guards. Ceres saw one cutting down a woman who had brought children with her, shoving her back into the crush.

Ceres braced herself. There came a point where she had to act even though it was suicidal. Where the only thing to do was to throw herself forward and hope. She took a breath, putting her hands on the nearest stones to pull herself through.

She only stopped when she heard the sound of horns, and saw the iron gates that led to the Stade's floor start to open.

"*More* soldiers?" she said to herself.

There were more soldiers, but not the ones she expected. Armored men charged into the Stade on horseback, with spears set for the impact of their assault. More followed, firing short bows as they rode, picking off archers on the other side and then whirling around as they drew their swords.

Ceres watched the remnants of Lord West's men slam into the Empire's soldiers and now her charge didn't seem so doomed after all.

"Up!" Ceres yelled to the combatlords. "There, we have to help them!"

Despite their wounds, despite their obvious exhaustion, the combatlords followed her, and Ceres felt a surge of pride in them for that. Without so much as a question, they moved in behind her, charging in a wedge of steel and muscle and violence.

While Lord West's contingent struck the Empire's soldiers from one side, Ceres and her combatlords hit them from the other. In the instant before they crashed into the imperial ranks, she had a moment to see the soldiers there torn with fear, unsure which opponent to face. Ceres even felt a moment of pity for them, there at the behest of an evil ruler without any kindness.

Then they crashed into them and there was no time to think about anything except the next blow, the next parry, the next flash of energy flickering out from her. In those first moments, it almost felt to Ceres as though she was clambering over a line of soldiers, running up a shield, then pushing off it to leap over the first rank of her enemies.

She landed in clear space, with imperial uniforms all around her. Ceres lashed out with both blades, keeping moving, not daring to stop. In that moment, she couldn't see her own side; it was as though she was lost in a forest, and every tree around her was a thing of sharp edges and evil intent.

Well, if she were in a forest, Ceres would just have to hack her way through.

She did, lashing out left and right, looking for any sign of her combatlords. She saw them, a trio of soldiers converging on one wielding a trident. Ceres stabbed one from behind, let the next step past her for the combatlord to cut down, then slammed into the third.

She saw the horsemen ahead and pointed to them. "Join up with Lord West's men!"

She wasn't sure if her words carried over the sounds of steel or the screams of the dying, but the men with her seemed to understand what she wanted. They cut their way through the men ahead of them, plunging on towards the mounted figures fighting beyond them.

They closed in toward each other, and somewhere in the middle, the Empire's soldiers broke. Some turned and ran, more threw themselves desperately at their new assailants. Neither worked. Ceres saw fleeing soldiers being dragged down by the crowd, their weapons quickly finding homes in new hands. She buried her own swords in the sand, willing to let others do this part.

In a matter of minutes, their last, desperate stand gave way to an arena where the only faces Ceres could see were friendly ones. The crowd were standing there, hefting their stolen prizes and cheering their success. Lord West's former men were circling, mopping up enemies, looking for any who might be waiting for them. Mostly, they rode with their pennants flying, looking every inch the glorious, victorious warriors they were.

Each group celebrated in their own ways. The combatlords roared and punched the air, saluting the crowd the way they might have after a particularly vicious Killing. The rebels there hugged one another, while the crowd shouted its approval.

"Ceres, Ceres, Ceres!"

Ceres stood there, taking it in, looking around at all of it.

142

She could feel the energy of the fight ebbing now. Probably soon, she would need to rest, to let her powers grow again. For now, it was over and—

Suddenly, a new legion of Empire soldiers marched into the Stade—more than had been there before. Ceres watched in dismay. They marched in step, utterly fresh—while Ceres and her forces were almost spent. Even the mounted soldiers of Lord West's forces looked exhausted.

They couldn't fight again.

And yet they would have to.

With the grim slowness of exhaustion, Ceres drew her blades up from the sand and prepared herself for the next confrontation.

One which, she knew, may very well be her last.

CHAPTER TWENTY NINE

Akila stood at the prow of his ship, watching with a growing sense of the rightness of it all as the city grew larger. Behind him sailed more ships, in the colors of imperial galleys.

"Be ready," he called back to his men. "They will have men on the docks, even if they believe we are their own, returned victorious from Haylon." He laughed. "Well, that part's true, at least."

He couldn't keep his sense of humor for long. This would be grim work. How many of his men would die here on this far shore? How much destruction would they cause in the name of freedom?

He found himself thinking back to the moments that had brought him there; that had convinced him to do this thing. When Thanos had come to them on Haylon, Akila had turned him away. He'd thought that the prince had merely wanted to use them to gain a kingdom.

I should have known better, Akila thought. *Thanos has more honor than that.*

If he'd realized it at the time, perhaps he would have sailed back with him. As it was, he'd driven Thanos away, and only realized the wrongness of what he was doing later, when he hadn't been able to sleep for thoughts of what he'd rejected.

The ships were getting closer now, pulling inside the limits of the harbor to clarion calls and the waving of flags. Akila watched tensely, waiting for the last of his ships to clear the line of the chains protecting the harbor.

They were almost at the dock now, and Akila raised his hand. *Be ready.*

The truly shaming thing had been the woman Thanos had brought with him to Haylon. She had been a prisoner, a self-confessed thief and worse, yet given the choice between following Thanos and forging a new life on Haylon, she had gone with the prince without even having to think about it. Honor had mattered more to her.

As it should have to me, Akila thought, in the instant before he let his hand fall.

"NOW!"

His men hauled on ropes, the colors on the mast changing, going from the red of the Empire to the blue of Haylon. Around him, he saw his other ships revealing their true purpose even as he felt the galley bump against the docks.

Ahead, he saw the city spread out before him. Smoke rising over the bulk of the Stade told him that they might have arrived just in time.

Akila drew his sword.

"Onward! To glory! To freedom!"

CHAPTER THIRTY

Ceres fought as though sleepwalking, her arm rising and falling almost mechanically. There were so many soldiers, and already, she could see those on her side falling.

She watched as one of Lord West's men was dragged from his horse, and the plunging blades brought back uncomfortable memories of all that had happened when they had assaulted the city.

Ceres shook her head, parried a blade, and struck back with enough force to behead an opponent.

I cannot let this happen again, Ceres told herself. *Not again.*

Images of Garrant's death came to her. Ceres pushed them aside and kept fighting, swinging her blades and keeping moving, even if she barely had the strength to do it. She wasn't going to stop. She wasn't going to let them die.

Except they were dying. Everywhere Ceres looked, people were dying. The spectators were dying in the stands. Lord West's men were dying on the sand. Even some of the combatlords were dying, brought down one by one by exhaustion and by weight of numbers despite their skills.

Ceres couldn't let it happen, whatever it took.

She reached into herself for the last of the strength that lay there. She drew it up, and then dragged more out of herself, despite the harm it would probably do to her. She didn't care if it killed her, so long as it helped to save some of those with her this time. She balled it up within her, ready to release it all in one last burst of force.

Only the sound of more horns stopped her.

Men ran into the Stade, and from the first, Ceres could see that they weren't more soldiers. They loped where the Empire's soldiers would have marched, running together while wearing colors Ceres vaguely recognized as those of Haylon.

They came, and *kept* coming, in numbers that seemed like enough to swamp the whole city. Ceres pushed the power back down inside her as they crashed into the Empire's soldiers, because she didn't need it now. This wasn't the time for sacrifice, but for action.

"One last push!" she yelled to her forces, making herself renew her assault on the soldiers in front of her.

She cut down one, then dove in front of another to block the strike he aimed at a combatlord. The heavily muscled fighter cut down the soldier with a blow from a short, stabbing spear.

"We need to fight *together*!" Ceres called out. Alone, they would be cut down. Together, they might just survive this.

She gathered the combatlords around her once more, preparing to continue the fight.

There was no need. The newcomers cut through the Empire's forces while barely slowing, their numbers and their ferocity adding neatly to that of those already there. Ceres saw the Empire's men stall in their attack, then turn and run, trying to find a way out of the Stade.

Those who could, ran. Those who couldn't, threw down their weapons.

Soon, all was still, as an eerie lull fell over the Stade.

Ceres watched as a wiry, commanding-looking man stepped out from the mass of the newcomers.

"I am Akila," he said. "Who commands here?"

Ceres managed to step up close to him, stumbling only slightly. "I'm Ceres."

She saw Akila looking her up and down. "*You're* Ceres? Thanos told me you were dead."

"Thanos?" Ceres repeated. "You've spoken to Thanos?"

"Not recently," Akila replied. "I'll tell you all of it soon. I guess we both have a lot to talk about. For now, though, the important part is that the battle here is over."

Ceres nodded, surveying the damage.

"It is."

It wasn't over, though, was it? There was still so much to do. There would be more soldiers in the rest of the city, and the castle would be hard to take.

She looked around the Stade, seeing the bodies there, the aftermath of the violence. She saw the fighters doubled over in exhaustion or pain, the ones who might never rise from where they lay.

They'd won, and it was exhilarating.

And yet, at the same time, the people were still not free. Their battle was just beginning.

CHAPTER THIRTY ONE

Lucious strode at the head of his mercenaries and thugs, royal guards following in their wake. He felt powerful, unbeatable. Invincible.

He felt free.

He should have killed his father years ago. All that time he'd been held back, reined in and controlled. He'd had to put up with lectures and commands, attempts to turn him into some storybook idea of a prince, and foolish ideas about honor that had nothing to do with reality.

Now, he didn't have to restrain himself. Now, he had soldiers at his back and the beginnings of an uprising to put down. He would slaughter his way through the peasants at the Stade, making a show out of them that people would remember for generations.

Perhaps he would have a statue made to commemorate it. Something that would make the pitiful busts in his father's chambers pale into insignificance. An image of himself bestriding a horde of slain rebels, perhaps, with adoring women looking up at him, grateful for the power of his rule. Perhaps he'd make Stephania pose for it. That would be amusing.

First, though, there was the matter of the Stade, although Lucious doubted that there would be that much to do when it came to the real fighting anymore. With all the soldiers he'd had sent to the Stade, even Ceres and her combatlords couldn't have survived.

No, if Lucious judged this right, he would arrive just in time to claim the glory and have his fun, without any real threat to himself. He would take what he wanted, the same way that he'd taken the Empire. He would show his fa—he would show the people of the Empire what a real king looked like, and they would bow down, or be made to.

"Looks like trouble up ahead," one of his men said.

Lucious looked toward the Stade, then waved that concern away. Yes, there was noise, and even smoke, but that was just the normal aftermath of a battle, wasn't it?

"It's nothing to worry about," Lucious said. "I sent enough soldiers into the Stade to take down a regiment. The last remnants of a broken rebellion are *nothing*."

Even so, he let the others go ahead of him. If there was nothing to worry about, he could still step to the fore. If there were still a few combatlords to finish, he could have the mercenaries bring them down with crossbows. Either way, there would be no problem.

It was only when he saw the crowds pouring out of the Stade that he started to realize that it might not have turned out the way he anticipated. He saw the soldiers in the uniforms of Lord West's men, resplendent in their armor, and his worry built—layer upon layer.

He narrowed his eyes, confused, and then spotted rebels wearing what he swore were the colors of Haylon—and fear bubbled up within him until it seemed to fill him to the brim.

He saw the combatlords pouring out from the Stade with the others, saw who stood at their heart—and his worry gave way to terror.

Ceres was alive, and she moved like the hero Lucious had wanted to be. Her blades were shining in her hands, and there was blood on them.

Lucious saw her turn, and he was sure that her eyes fixed on him. She shouldn't have been able to pick him out at that distance, but he was sure that she did, just as he was sure about the malevolence there that turned her from someone in the midst of celebration to some kind of instrument of vengeance.

He had a moment to think that maybe golden armor wasn't the best way to blend in.

And then he saw Ceres gesture and the crowd surge forward.

Right toward him.

His fear bubbled over into panic, but he managed enough control to turn to the others and point at the advancing horde.

"What are you waiting for? Slaughter those peasants! Charge!"

Some of them did; yet more of them did not.

Lucious didn't care either way, because he was already running.

He glanced back just long enough to see the first of his men being cut down, and they didn't even seem to slow the wash of people descending on them. They poured over his mercenaries like the rising tide, cutting them down or simply trampling them. There were simply too many of them.

Lucious ran faster then, really ran. One of his men got in the way and Lucious elbowed him aside, not caring that he heard the man scream and fall just behind him.

He ran down a side street, breaking away from the main avenue leading to the Stade. There was still the sound of footsteps behind him, and Lucious felt a hand grabbing for his shoulder. He drew a blade and stabbed back without pausing, not caring if it was one of the rebels or one of his own soldiers who had grabbed him. He felt the blade slide into flesh and kept moving.

Lucious kept running, his brain working on pure instinct as he picked turnings to dart down. He'd learned a surprising amount about the layout of the city in his days ravaging it and taking Stephania's informants from her, but even so, he quickly found himself getting lost.

Maybe that was a good thing. If he didn't know where he was, how could anybody else find him? Even so, he kept running until his heart hammered in his chest and his breath seemed to burn every time he drew it in. That didn't take long. Lucious had never been one to put himself through unnecessary exercise.

He broke open a door at random, his sword out to gut any occupants of the hovel he found himself in before they could attract attention. It was empty though. Comfortingly empty and dark, with light only coming in through the slats of boarded up windows.

Lucious pushed the door closed and leaned against it, not wanting to sit down on a floor covered with filthy straw, or even risk the few ragged pieces of furniture that remained there.

"How?" he demanded of the empty air. "How could this happen?"

He did it quietly, though, because there was still too much of a risk that someone might be outside, searching for him.

He needed a way out of the city. His men had been cut to pieces. The soldiers in the city had almost certainly been slaughtered as well, because the peasants wouldn't have emerged from the Stade so easily if it hadn't been the case.

There were probably those who thought that Lucious was stupid. That he was no kind of strategist. His father certainly had, before he'd learned better. But Lucious could see which way the wind was blowing, and you didn't need to be much of a strategist to know that it wasn't possible to hold a city without an army.

Which meant but one thing: he needed to get out of Delos.

Methodically, Lucious started to remove his armor, stripping down to his tunic and hose. Even that wouldn't be good enough, because the quality of them would be far too recognizable. So he went around the hovel, searching until he came up with rags in which to dress. He put them on over his tunic, of course. He didn't want the things touching his skin, after all.

He smeared his golden hair with dirt to complete the impression of one of the lower orders, and stashed his sword in a burlap sack.

As he took a deep breath and stepped into the street, Lucious felt sure that every eye was upon him, and that the hordes of rebels would descend upon him. Around him, Lucious could hear the shouts and cries of rebellion, smell the scent of burning that always came with such things.

Yet no one came for him.

When he walked past a group of rioters, they barely gave him a second glance. People had spent so long seeing him in his finery that without it, he was almost invisible. If his face hadn't been streaked with dirt, Lucious might almost have appreciated that.

He couldn't go to the docks. If there were rebels from Haylon there, that meant ships, probably enough to hunt down any imperial vessel trying to leave. There were other ways, though.

Lucious hunted through the streets until he found what he'd been searching for, what his traitors and informants had told him all about.

The entrance to the rebellion's tunnels was hidden at the back of an inn, behind a wooden wheel half collapsed against a wall. He ducked into the dark, finding a candle hidden there and lighting it. There was a certain poetry to using this way out of the city.

Lucious looked back, seeing the castle away in the distance. He wondered if it would be alight soon, and how many of those there the rebels would kill in their marauding through the city. He found that he didn't care, even when it occurred to him that his mother was still in there. The only thing that did matter was what it said about him. The Year Long King? Lucious hadn't managed more than an hour yet, and already he'd lost his capital city.

I'll get it back.

That would be easy enough. Delos was just one city, and he was the rightful heir to the Empire. An empire that had soldiers everywhere, way outside these city walls, in its farthest reaches. An empire that had allies and client states, old friends and countries that owed them favors.

Felldust, he thought, the shape of the plan already forming in his mind. They were some of the Empire's closest allies, with long links to their houses. He would head down the coast until he found a fishing village, hire passage on a boat, and only announce himself when he got there. Once he did, it would only take one conversation with their rulers before they gave him their support.

Their support—and more importantly, their army.

Lucious nodded to himself as he took one last look at the city. A city that was falling to pieces even while he waited.

I will return, he thought. *And I will take it back.*

COMING SOON!

Book #5 in Of Crowns and Glory

Books by Morgan Rice

THE WAY OF STEEL
ONLY THE WORTHY (BOOK #1)

VAMPIRE, FALLEN
BEFORE DAWN (BOOK #1)

OF CROWNS AND GLORY
SLAVE, WARRIOR, QUEEN (BOOK #1)
ROGUE, PRISONER, PRINCESS (BOOK #2)
KNIGHT, HEIR, PRINCE (BOOK #3)
REBEL, PAWN, KING (BOOK #4)
SOLDIER, BROTHER SORCERER (BOOK #5)

KINGS AND SORCERERS
RISE OF THE DRAGONS
RISE OF THE VALIANT
THE WEIGHT OF HONOR
A FORGE OF VALOR
A REALM OF SHADOWS
NIGHT OF THE BOLD

THE SORCERER'S RING
A QUEST OF HEROES
A MARCH OF KINGS
A FATE OF DRAGONS
A CRY OF HONOR
A VOW OF GLORY
A CHARGE OF VALOR
A RITE OF SWORDS
A GRANT OF ARMS
A SKY OF SPELLS
A SEA OF SHIELDS
A REIGN OF STEEL
A LAND OF FIRE
A RULE OF QUEENS
AN OATH OF BROTHERS
A DREAM OF MORTALS
A JOUST OF KNIGHTS

THE GIFT OF BATTLE

About Morgan Rice

Morgan Rice is the #1 bestselling and USA Today bestselling author of the epic fantasy series THE SORCERER'S RING, comprising seventeen books; of the #1 bestselling series THE VAMPIRE JOURNALS, comprising twelve books; of the new vampire series VAMPIRE, FALLEN; of the #1 bestselling series THE SURVIVAL TRILOGY, a post-apocalyptic thriller comprising three books; of the #1 bestselling epic fantasy series KINGS AND SORCERERS, comprising six books; of the new epic fantasy series THE WAY OF STEEL; and of the new epic fantasy series OF CROWNS AND GLORY. Morgan's books are available in audio and print editions, and translations are available in over 25 languages.

Morgan loves to hear from you, so please feel free to visit www.morganricebooks.com to join the email list, receive a free book, receive free giveaways, download the free app, get the latest exclusive news, connect on Facebook and Twitter, and stay in touch!

CPSIA information can be obtained
at www.ICGtesting.com
Printed in the USA
LVOW13s1112290317
528894LV00018B/351/P